Created, Written, and Illustrated by
DONALD "SCRIBE" ROSS

DEDICATED TO MY FAMILY FOR ALWAYS
SUPPORTING ME IN MY DREAMS.

THE RESOUND FIELDS
Copyright © 2022 Donald "Scribe" Ross. All rights reserved.

Published by Outland Entertainment LLC
3119 Gillham Road
Kansas City, MO 64109

Founder/Publisher: Jeremy D. Mohler
Editor-in-Chief: Alana Joli Abbott

ISBN: 978-1-954255-49-4
eBook ISBN: 978-1-954255-53-1
Worldwide Rights
Created in the United States of America

Developmental Editor: Alana Joli Abbott
Copyeditor: Scott Colby
Cover & Interior Illustration: Donald "Scribe" Ross
Fiber & Plush Characters: Alisa Ross
Logo Design: Tuke (@tuke_df)
Cover & Book Design: Jeremy D. Mohler

Printed and bound in China.

Visit outlandentertainment.com to see more, or follow us on our Facebook Page facebook.com/outlandentertainment/

TABLE of CONTENTS

CHAPTER 1

A DAY OFF OR AN OFF DAY?

A verdant spring morning dawned over the midtown section of Kansas City, Missouri. Inside a small studio apartment on the second floor, the morning light worked its way through the cracks of the shades. Soft blues and purples worked their way around the room, eventually landing on a large rhinoceros curled up in bed.

Rumpus, the rhino in question, was an artist trying to find his way—but he wasn't very excited about getting up for work. The light landed on his face, making his eyes squish and squeeze until a sliver revealed a small part of his off-white eye. His blue pupil raised into position like the morning sun.

"Oh God," he groaned. "I really don't think I can do another day at that stupid job."

As he sat up in bed, his shoulder drooped in defeat, and he slumped over. Rumpus reached over to grab his cell phone just as the annoying chime of his alarm went off. He swiped to shut it off and dialed his work number, practicing a believable cough. It wasn't hard to summon up a sad voice, but Rumpus dropped it a couple octaves to leave a message.

"Hey, Bill," he said, coughing and then clearing his throat. "I'm sorry, man, but I'm not going to be able to make it into work today." He groaned for good measure. It wasn't hard to fake. "My stomach is all jacked up, and I am worried about getting sick at work. I'll call you this afternoon and let you know what's up with tomorrow." He coughed, and his voice grumbled as he said, "Thanks."

He disconnected and breathed a sigh of relief. Now Rumpus had something to look forward to. "I think," he began, his voice rising in a melodic tone, "today is a good day to go take pictures of graffiti!" He swung out of bed and swayed his hips in delight. "I heard Quisp did a new piece down in Brush Creek, and it's only a short bus ride away."

Rumpus flicked over to his music app and set the speaker above the vanity to play his latest Joc Max funk and soul mix. Joc rarely liked people to record his sets, but a mutual friend, Dani Girl, occasionally managed to weasel her way to recording one. In a cloud of steam and soul, Rumpus climbed into the shower, soaking for way too long, imagining himself washing off all the mundane and repetitive interactions of the previous day. He grabbed a poor breakfast of the previous night's pizza and coffee from Minsky's, packed his backpack with his sketchbook and phone charger, and headed out of his small apartment perched on the second floor.

There was always something special about taking the bus. Rumpus felt at peace when he had his headphones in and could watch the city roll by, like he was riding in a gentle beast floating on migration to another part of the world. The constant energy of people living their lives was both an amazing feeling and overwhelming to him. One day, he would experience it with fascination, and the next, it would freak him out to just think about how many people and creatures really lived out there in the world. His mind wandered until the driver sounded the announcement: "47th and Broadway, Plaza stop." Rumpus exited the bus, made his way past the tennis players, and ambled down the hill into the dried-out flood drainage area known as Brush Creek.

Brush Creek was one of his favorite places to hang out. He would wander from one end of the plaza toward a place known as "The Paseo," a group of three dirty, long tunnels under Paseo Avenue. Painters, both professionals and amateurs, frequently gathered there during the day to paint. Rumpus saw Sebastian playing his saxophone in the middle, where the ceiling curved upward into a large concrete dome that carried the sound right into his bones. They never spoke to each other, but there seemed to be an understanding Rumpus had with him. Both of them were practicing their art in a special place, and that was all that they needed to know about each other. Rumpus had played sax in the past and sold it before going to school, a decision he seemed to regret from time to time. As he passed, he nodded to Sebastian.

Rumpus hopped back and forth over the drainage ditch flowing with water from the affluent Mission Hills, grimacing at all the trash that collected in the branches. People had left all types of personal items in a collage of discarded background stories. The Paseo was pretty gross, and the garbage made it difficult to paint. But what option did you have when you lived in a city that didn't support mural work of any kind? You fit in where you felt like you fit in. Rumpus wondered if that was what Sebastian felt, too.

The sounds of Zero 7 gently flowed through a set of headphones on ears that seemed too small for Rumpus's bulky head. Violins and a heavy bassline set the pace of his impenetrable feet. He walked toward the east end and nostalgically noticed old tags of East and Krie, the bubble letters faded from big washouts during flooding times.

"I need to get out and paint more," he muttered to himself. Rumpus turned back to look at Sebastian, hoping the musician heard him and was going to slide him a nod of agreement, but Sebastian, his eyes closed, was in his own his own colorful cloud of sounds and musical storytelling. "That's a time when I feel the most free—or *felt* the most free. It sures seems like forever ago."

Rumpus couldn't really afford paint with his job, and he definitely couldn't afford to make bad decisions. He was on the tail end of a three-year probation, an excessive punishment for poor choices—stealing and worse—when he was eighteen. It had forever changed his life and altered a lot of his original dreams; he'd been pushed underground, like Sebastian's saxophone.

Just as his mind started to wander down a rabbit hole of self-pity, his thoughts were cut off by a change of scenery. The new Quisp piece he had heard about was there, still untouched by the little wannabe gangster kids that also visited the tunnels. The sun's glare made the paint still look wet, and Rumpus took in a deep breath, as if he could still smell the paint fumes.

All he smelled was sour water and trash. *Amazing,* he thought. "It's cool to still see full color pieces where you could tell someone passionately put it out there, not expecting a return," he said aloud, raising his phone to take a picture. Street art was changing around him, and Rumpus was a romantic about changes in the scene.

The sound of rocks falling interrupted his thoughts, and Rumpus found himself squinting into the darkest shadow of the tunnel. There was a long pause, and even the wind around him and the leaves on the trees stopped moving as if all of them together were curious about the same thing.

This may sound weird for the location—but maybe not, considering all the gross stuff on the ground around him. A massive squishy, low thud hit the ground, and a small shockwave vibrated under Rumpus's feet. The sound of more rocks and wet slaps froze Rumpus in his tracks. He stared back into the mouth of the tunnel and started building an image of something huge back in the inky darkness. But how could that be? He'd just walked through there, and the faint music of the saxophone continued, uninterrupted. Was it some kind of earthquake? Kansas City didn't have those, did they? Chunks of rock broke loose from the cement bridge railing and fell toward the ground on the center tunnel; a small dust cloud rolled out like a hot breath past his weary feet.

A man ran to the southern side of the bridge, stealing Rumpus's focus from the inside of the tunnel. "At least I know it's not only in my mind," he muttered.

Rumpus stood in silence for a moment, waiting for what might be coming next, but there was nothing.

My mind must be playing tricks on me because I'm still stressed about my probation.

He knew there were sewer pipes in the tunnels; there must be something happening elsewhere that rattled all drain run-off pipes leading in there. Who knew what it could be in this area? Maybe part of the construction projects planned to permanently fill Brush Creek with water, making his favorite walks through this old street art gallery a thing of the past. Rumpus sighed as he looked back down at the camera on his phone. "What a shame," he said aloud.

Sometimes I wish I could just be taken away from all of this... It seems like everything I love the most fades away or is taken from me as I get older, year after year...just like my grandfather too.

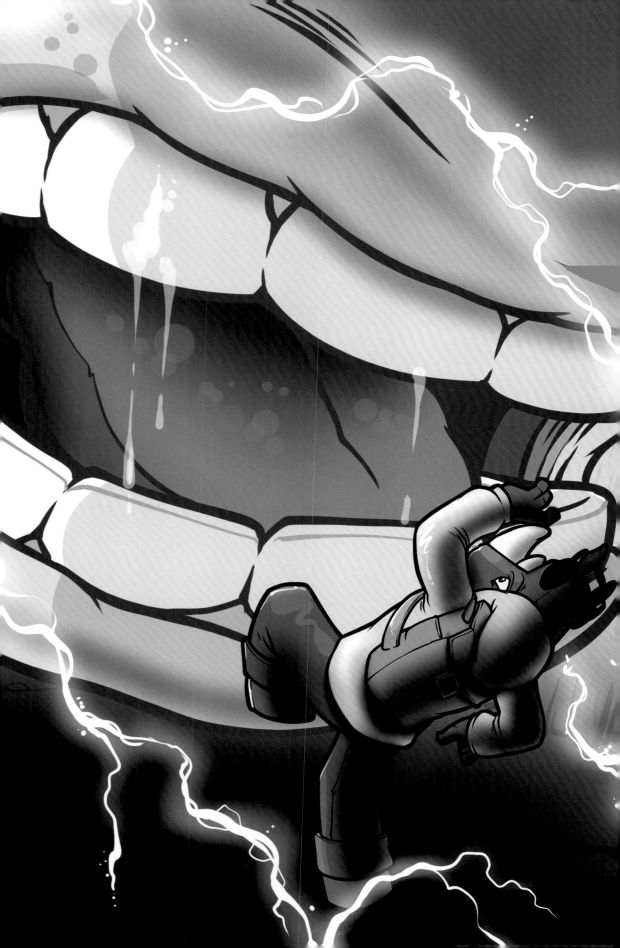

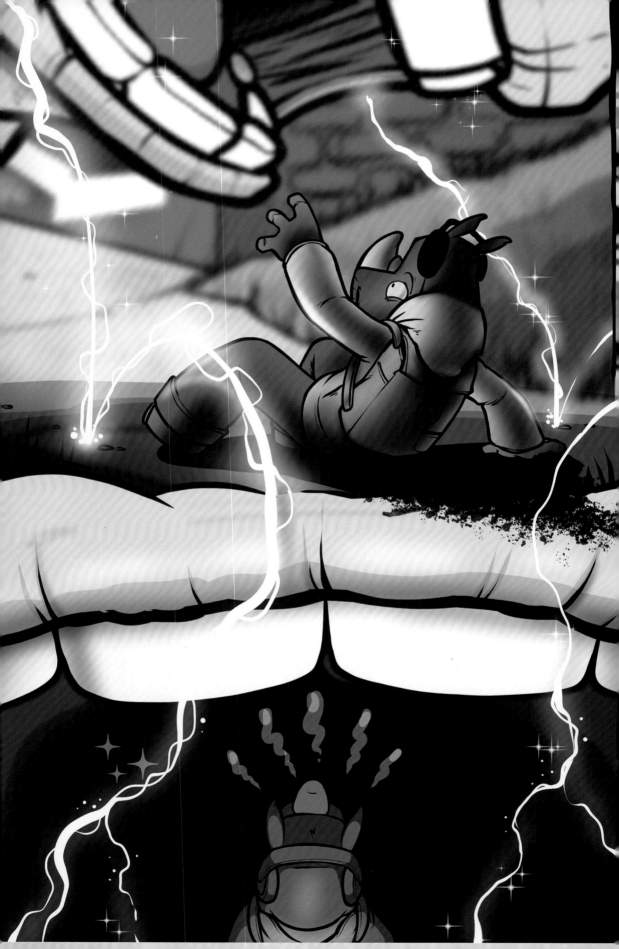

CHAPTER 2

A WHALE OF A TALE

Inside the whale, Rumpus sat in the dark, wondering where he was going and if he would even be alive in several hours.

What am I inside of? he wondered.

"Why ME!!" he screamed out. "That's what I get for taking the day off, I guess," he whispered. A frightened laugh bubbled out of him, and he wished he'd never called out sick.

Moments later, a window opened from what looked like the end of a large room. Was he being summoned to go in that direction—and did he have a choice? His eyes started to adjust to the wildflower-blue light at the end of the expanse. Ribs led up to a giant spine on the ceiling of this cathedral-like space. The floor under his feet was soft, reminding him of the squishy floors at playgrounds, and he made his way slowly to the window. He reached out cautiously to the portal and pulled his eye up to the window vibrating in prisms of light.

Awe and confusion came over him as a swirling tunnel of colors focused into a peephole into the place he worked. His fellow employees were working away in a desaturated funk; as usual, no one looked very happy except for Alphonso. Rumpus had suspicions on why that guy was always happy. Alphonso always smelled interesting when he came back from his car on break. Their manager barked orders; people shuffled about like zombies in a bad movie, the brown boxes and grey floors a reflection of the depressing atmosphere.

"You know… this situation is really scary, and I might die, but I feel like I was already half dead in that place," he whispered to himself.

Just then the window slammed shut, vibrations echoing off the walls around him, leaving him in the dark again.

After what seemed like hours, Rumpus remembered his phone.

Maybe I could call for help, he thought.

Where would I tell them to go, though? Look for the giant whale?

He ran a thumb over the screen.

Besides, looks like I have no bars.

At least he could listen to some music. He plugged in his headphones and leaned on his backpack, using it like a pillow. His big thumb scrolled through his tracklist and landed on a song by Lee Dorsey. He couldn't think of a more perfect song than "Who's Gonna Help Brother Get Further."

The music played, and Rumpus thought about his family and friends.

"I might not ever see my family again, and I'm going to be missing just like Grandpa Duncan," he said on an exhale. A tear rolled down his tough leather cheek when another window opened at the other side of the room. This time Rumpus scrambled to his feet and ran over to see what it might be.

This window showed Rumpus the front of his parents' house, looking like a washed-out old home movie—but it warmed his heart. His Grandpa Duncan was pulling up to the house in his old Shelby GT350. This was an old memory of the many times his grandpa came to take him out. His mom was sending out a twelve-year-old Rumpus to the museum with Grandpa Duncan. "This was the last day I saw Grandpa Duncan," he said as tears streaked down his face. This window stayed

open much longer than the last one. Rumpus got to relive that whole day as they went to the museum to look at Grandpa's favorite works by Fredrick Remmington and Thomas Hart Benton.

"I was born in the wrong era, I think," his grandpa said to him, and it echoed through the cavern. It was something Rumpus could relate to even more now that he was older. "When I was growing up, all I thought about was traveling the Wild West and sketching what I saw." Young Rumpus looked up to his grandfather with admiration dancing in his blue eyes.

"I could go with you too, Grandpa," he said.

"I could think of nothing better, little man…"

The words echoed through the cavern as Grandpa Duncan looked at the Rumpus in the window with a loving gaze. The window started to close. "NNNNNOOOOO!!" screamed Rumpus. He slammed his hands against the window, trying to keep it open to no avail. He slid to his knees, pounding the floor in anger. On his hands and knees, he looked to the roof in the darkness.

"Why are you doing this to me?" he belted out. His head drooped down and he sobbed, his voice trembling as he asked, "Who are you? What is this?"

Rumpus sniffed, and when his pleas were met only with silence, he screamed out, "Tell me what is going on, damn it!"

The screen of his phone came on suddenly, and he reached for it, pulling the headphone back to his ear. "New World in my View" by King Britt and Sister Gertrude Morgan played, and Rumpus sat in the dark and cried.

Time slowly passed. His phone finally died right as the third window started to open, halfway between the two he had previously looked through. He ran over, and the swirl of light he saw at the beginning of each of the other openings didn't stop. A spiral of light and what looked like dye pushing through water in a rainbow of colors spun the living cavern around him. It reminded him of the tunnel in *Willy Wonka*. "What is this supposed to be he?" he demanded of the darkness. "This doesn't help at all."

If someone had been flying next to the whale, on the outside, they'd be able to see the creature was speeding down a giant wormhole of light—but the swarm of bees had caught up to them and was stinging the whale all over his body. That observer could certainly hear Rumpus's muffled screams, though in polite company, the observer certainly wouldn't repeat every word he was shouting.

Inside the beast, Rumpus banged on the windowpane one more time, which alerted one of the bees to the window's location.

In a flash, a large, yellow face appeared in the window, its eyes pressed firmly to the glass with its pupil twitching in a circular motion, trying to see who might be inside. The pupil locked in on Rumpus, and the vessel shook, swinging back and forth, smashing the bees against the walls of the wormhole. The thrashing intensified as sparks and light strobed through the window.

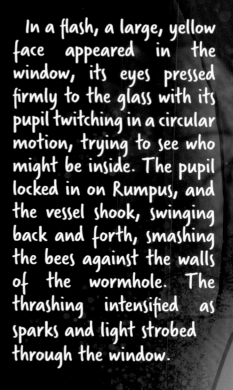

Rumpus could now sort of see the jawbone and teeth off in the distance—and SMASH! He was launched into the air, hitting his head on a rib bone. The crash left him knocked out and lying on the floor. The window closed above his head, and he was returned to darkness.

It's hard to say how long Rumpus lay there. Does time even work normally when you are riding in the belly of a giant whale and traveling down a wormhole? The rest of the ride was smooth, and Rumpus didn't feel a thing. It was probably the best sleep he'd had in months, which was the first upside to the situation. He dreamed like he was back at his childhood home, and this had never happened. He dreamed a very circular dream in which his entire encounter with the whale had been a nightmare.

At the other end of the wormhole was a field of tall grass. A wind gently blew the tall blades, and bird song trilled in the distance. A strange bug with six eyes cleaned its face on a twig; its wings popped up, and with a buzzing hum, it flew away.

Despite the clear skies, the grass pulled toward the distance, as though caught in a blustery wind. A hole pulled the sky open; nearby clouds caught in its gravity, swirling around the hole and bumping into each other, hot and cold air sending lightning cascading to the ground and to the edges of the hole.

In a flash, the whale appeared with a calm and collected smile, hovering above the grass pushed down in a crop-circle pattern. A ring of smoke rose from the circle's edge, and a loud sound—like a speaker getting feedback—blew out in every direction. The whale looked around with his kind eyes, searching for bees that might have followed him through. He cleared his throat, cheeks going up and down, the skin behind his head contracting like an accordion. Fat rolls rippled across his body, as though he were trying to force something from the lowest part of his stomach. He rolled his eyes back to sneeze…

With a series of wet, burp-like sounds, lips rolling like a crowd doing the wave at a sporting event, the whale opened his cavernous mouth, tongue rolled out like a carpet. A small, passed out Rumpus flicked from the end of the tongue, right onto the middle of the soft, patterned grass.

Once again, the birds began to chirp, and the wind returned to a normal summer breeze.

CHAPTER 3

RESOUND FIELDS WELCOME WAGON

Rumpus lay on the ground in the warm sun. He was afraid to open his eyes, instead letting his ears tune into the sounds around him. The longer he listened to the nearby wildlife singing in the wind, the more it sounded like they were creating a song together. He could hear the really low breathing of a massive animal next to him. He could feel slime all over his body as he raised his hand to wipe his eyes and focus on his abductor from the graffiti tunnels.

It was a massive floating whale!!!

His eyes couldn't believe it. Was he dreaming? He looked past the whale to take in more of his surroundings, noting a small lake in the distance and the purple mountain range.

Rumpus started to get to his feet as the slime dripped off his limbs, pulling his backpack back onto his shoulders. He locked eyes again with this

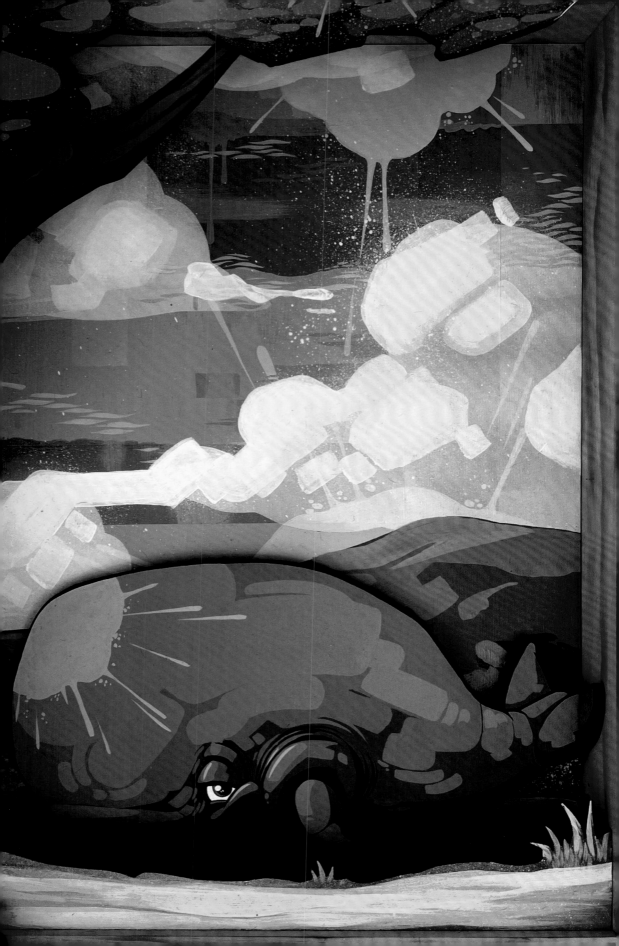

gentle giant, who smiled at him kindly. He must have started to feel a little bit more comfortable, because he blurted out, "Man, I almost don't want to wake up from this dream! Or at least I—"

As soon as his eyes left the whale, he was blasted by a surprise eruption of fish breath. The sudden

gust had him leaning back and swinging his arms to keep his balance as the slime flew right off him. He slowly thumped onto his butt, and when he looked up again the whale was gone.

"What the—"

Rumpus was cut off by a voice behind him. "Now *that* is a big deal, son." Rumpus spun to find an even stranger creature looking at him. It had four near-ungulate legs, a lizard-like tail with an egg-shaped body, and two long ape arms. Its head had four eyes, a mane of luxurious hair, and horse ears.

Rumpus jumped as the creature spoke again. "I mean seeeriously. You get dropped off by the transporter, Sheol, aaaand get washed clean? Man, you must be the real thing. Or he really likes you, buddy."

"Sheol?" Rumpus asked in doubt. "What is a Sheol?"

The creature laughed at him. "Only the freshest transporter in history. I can't even count how many moon cycles it's been since we saw him around these parts. It's been so long that some of the newer creatures here think he's just a myth. This is a good day, my friend—a special day. The dude has been known to be super picky about who he brings here."

"Where is here?" asked Rumpus. "What is this place?"

The creature grinned, his six eyes gleaming. "You are standing in Resound Fields, the grooviest part of the island known as Nisamehe."

Resound Fields

The rhinoceros looked down at his feet "I don't understand why I am here."

Taking a step back to look up to him, the creature answered, "Sheol has always been involved in some of the biggest events on this island…" The strange creature's tail swished behind him. "To be honest, I hope this means that things are changing around here. We could use some change around this place." He grinned again. "So where are you from?"

Not making eye contact, Rumpus sheepishly answered, "KC. Kansas City. In Missouri."

"Misery? You must be glad not to be there anymore, then," the creature chuckled as he stepped into Rumpus's shadow.

The big rhino actually smiled. "No, Miss-our-i—but you sort of told a joke often said back home."

The creature poked Rumpus in the chest playfully. "You sure do remind me of me of El Vaquero. Kind of like a younger version of him, in fact—"

"Well, I don't know who that is," Rumpus cut him off. "Is there a way for me to find this Sheol whale so I can talk to…"

The creature's huge hand flew to Rumpus's mouth, silencing him. "Shhh, do you hear that?" Rumpus listened hard, but all he heard were the birds and insects around them. "Whatever you do, remember this one thing," the creature continued. "Do. Not. Eat. The cupcakes here."

He took his hand off Rumpus's mouth, and the rhino started to turn in a circle, scanning the landscape until he was back around to what he thought was facing the creature. The mysterious figure was gone.

What in the world is up with everyone vanishing in this place? he wondered.

They seem to leave as fast as they show up.

Rumpus looked in every direction, taking several steps one way, then several steps in another, but he just couldn't seem to make up his mind where to go. In one direction were fields as far as the eyes could see, broken only by an occasional tree. Another direction featured the purple mountains, but it looked as if he would never get there. A small body of water stood not too far away, so he decided to get a drink while he figured out his next steps.

When Rumpus got to the edge of the lake, he found a log to sit on where he could think for a minute. Strange bugs and creatures moved around him in curiosity, but Rumpus was too lost in thought to notice. They slowly started to surround him, taking turns looking from behind leaves and peeking from behind bushes. Even the plant life had turned in Rumpus's direction, but as soon as Rumpus started to look around, the plants straightened up and the creatures dispersed.

One of the creatures summoned up some bravery and came out to sniff his finger. A little taken aback, Rumpus pulled his hand away—but then slowly reached out. The insect rubbed up against his finger. With a trill of purring noises in three octaves, the bug rubbed its feathery fur apart against Rumpus's fingernail.

This place reminds me of the Flint Hills in Kansas with all the tall grass—but we are definitely not in Kansas anymore.

While Rumpus contemplated the situation, someone watched him from the water, hiding behind reeds in the distance. Had Rumpus been paying attention, he might have seen a party hat balanced above a set of goofy eyes breaking the water. Under the water, a set of tusks and bristled muzzle released bubbles to the surface.

Curious, the creature thought.

This guy looks a lot like El Vaquero. I should report to General Von Hareliar. It has been a long time since we had a visitor in the Fields, and I bet my reward will buy a lot of party time—and cupcakes!

CHAPTER 4

CAN A WALRUS WEAR A PARTY HAT?

Walrusamus was actually a good dude once you got to know him. Though he had a big heart, he'd gone through a lot in his life, which had led to a nervous breakdown. He loved his cupcakes, and providing information to the general got him many shipments of his favorite treats: cupcakes and fizzwizzle drinks. Some around the island called him Party Walrus; he never seemed to take off his party hat and was perpetually in the middle of something fun, with plenty of cupcakes to give away. The parties yielded Walrusamus a lot of accidental information, which he transmitted to the general and his goons from his base under the water of Lake Tafadhali. He was stationed near the Resound Fields partially to keep an eye on the area, since that was the last place Sheol had dropped off a visitor, eight years prior to the arrival of Rumpus.

This Life of the Party Walrus was one of the few that had experienced the legend of El Vaquero. Walrusamus had mixed feelings about him, but he had mixed feelings about his obligations to the powers that be on the island, too. The memory of this legend for most was beginning to fade—minus the inhabitants closest to El Vaquero, and those that hated him. El Vaquero had caused a pretty good stir leading up to the great war known as the Desert Feud. Walrusamus had met him a few times and actually got along with Vaquero, but he was following orders, and cupcakes were just too irresistible to him.

Across the lake, Rumpus knelt, looking at his reflection and cupping water to his dry mouth. He noticed a party hat floating on the top of the water, zigzagging toward him. "This has got to be the strangest place on earth," he muttered, "or wherever I am." As he spoke, a squatty walrus with a party hat and a rubber suit emerged and waddled from the water. Rumpus shook his head. "I would say that each thing that happens is a surprise, but the weirdness is starting to feel normal."

As soon as his head was out of the water, Party Walrus rattled off an introduction in a used-car-salesman voice.

Rumpus stepped back, irritated by what seemed like half-drunk close talk. "Why would I know what is going on?" Rumpus countered. "I don't even know where this place is! Seems like you know a lot more about why I might be here with all those specific questions. I just want to find my way home."

Adjusting his invisible bow tie and flicking his party hat, the goofball tried his best to summon a lucid and normal answer. "Well then, just slow down and have a listen—pay attention, my friend. Start walking west from here and along the way, ask anyone you see where Greedy Hedo is. He owns a great place down at Port Croon. He can put you in touch with all the right people to get home—if that is what you really want. There are small boats to take you out of Limerick Cove to where the big ships are. They'll take you anywhere you would like to go. Along the way, you might encounter a possible cupcake hopping around. Don't be alarmed! Our all-knowing president, Mr. Omega, has them placed around the island to care for his supporters. He saved the island years ago

by providing us with such food, so feel free to take advantage."

As fast as he'd showed up, Party Walrus swirled an about-face and shuffled back into the water with a sense of pride at how clever he was.

Reaching out toward the walrus's back, Rumpus could barely get out, "Wait! I need—"

With his back to Rumpus, Walrusamus yelled out right before he submerged, "Don't forget! Head west, cupcakes are good, and we will see you again! I'm off to work!"

SPLASH!

Rumpus stared out into the water, blinking. He finally broke the silence, complaining, "Before I even had a chance to ask him which way west was, this guy takes off."

Raising his horn to the sky, he thought maybe looking at the sun would give him a feeling of direction, but there were two of them. Once again, he was left with the choice of which direction to go.

Below the surface of the water, Party Walrus made his way back to his hiding place in the reeds. A bee flew up behind him and hovered by his shoulder. "I want you to fly as fast as you can and take a message to the General," Walrusamus ordered.

"Yes sir!" buzzed the bee.

"The message is this: we have a new visitor on the island brought here by Sheol. Before you head to the capital, I need you to swing west and tell Baker 8 to make as many cupcakes as he can and get them out into the wild. We need to get this guy plugged into the system as soon as we can. He needs to be ready to meet Mr. Omega."

Since Rumpus didn't know where to start and had no sense of which direction was west, he figured it best to follow the direction his horn was pointing. He headed west completely accidentally.

Watching from behind his reeds, Party Walrus assumed that all things were in place. He dunked his head back down into the water and swam away.

Then the breeze picked up, blowing another direction, and the tall grass pointed the way. The tufts on the tops of the grass almost all looked like a bunch of hands pointing. Rumpus noticed it and thought,

Well that seems like as good a direction as any!

It felt like the first time something made sense to him, so he went with it.

Rumpus turned to the right, took a deep breath, and figured that at least walking out into the fields would give him the chance to see if anyone was coming. In the distance, tucked under the leaves high up in a tree, another creature watched Rumpus, its rainbow of feathers glimmering in the afternoon sun.

CHAPTER 5

GRASS ROOTS

The cautious rhino walked through the tall grass for a few miles, looking up occasionally at the twin suns. Little did he know that on the island, looking up at the sun for direction was useless. Most of the inhabitants didn't know this, but the Island of Nisamehe floated on the back of a giant sea turtle. The random rumble the residents would call an earthquake was just the turtle eating—or maybe it had an itch. There were three islands on this small water world. It wasn't like Earth with all its land masses. The people on the island had never been able to figure out why they could sometimes see another island off in the distance, but then the next day it was gone. It might show up on the other side of the island months later. Days and nights changed their lengths, so time flowed strangely. Sometimes, when the other island was visible, pirates that harbored in Limerick Cove would occasionally get brave and sail toward it, while another member of the crew would monitor the distance, making sure they could always get home.

No one could chart the stars to an island on the move. How could you use the sun or stars on an island that is slowly moving around? But of course, Rumpus didn't know this. All he knew from his short, weird experiences so far was that this wasn't home, and he needed to try his best to avoid having expectations rooted in the world he understood. Riding in a giant whale had blown his mind—it changed his perspective on things.

As Rumpus walked, he noticed the sound of water nearby, which broke the monotony of the ocean of wild grass. Despite the strangeness, he was falling in love with the place; a great sense of peace washed over him. When he traveled out of Kansas City to the Flint Hills in Kansas, he would just sit out there for hours. Where he was walking felt special; it felt like there was lost history. It was peaceful, but missing something too.

He was getting thirsty. The grass was up to his waist, and he could only hear the water. Narrowing his eyes, Rumpus tried to focus on where the sound was coming from when a flash of color caught his attention. The flash landed in the same direction as the sound, so now Rumpus had two reasons to explore that way. "Looks like I might not be the only one that is thirsty," he said cheerfully. As he moved closer, the trickle of the water turned into the light melody of someone humming a tune. "Here we go again," he chuckled to himself.

"Hello!... Heeeellllooo? Is someone there?" someone yelled out from the direction Rumpus was heading.

"Uuuummmm, hello?" Rumpus called back. "I come in peace. My name is R—"

From the bushes came a happy yell. "Well get over here my friend! I have been waiting for you, Rumpus!"

Was it someone he'd already met? Maybe it was the strange creature from right after the whale dropped him off. But the voice didn't sound like someone he knew, so how did it know his name?

Rumpus stumbled forward into a lion basking in the sun like he didn't have a care in the world. His mane was a golden clay brown, and he wore a three-striped fuzzy headband. Hair covered his eyes, but the way his mane rolled off to the sides, the hair itself appeared like blissful closed eyes. The lion's mouth looked stuck in a perma-grin, and his tail twitched with excitement. Rumpus glanced down at the lion's foot and noticed a shackle on his furry ankle, with a chain running to the large rock he was leaning on.

"Oh, don't worry about that big fella," the lion said. "I just let them put that on me so they think they're in charge." He leaned a little closer to Rumpus, whispering, "It's important for those who want to be in control to *think* they are. The cupcakes aren't the only thing on the island that give people what they want."

The lion started to laugh and giggle. Rumpus looked back down at the shackle again and wondered why. Was this creature a madman or a convict of sorts, left out to die?

The lion spoke up again. "I promise, son, these chains cannot hold me. I promise you don't have to worry about me. I'm just an

old man who wanders these parts and was chained here for talking about what freedom is. Sit down, big Rumpus, and get yourself a drink from this sweet creek. Replenish your body and let it reach your soul. Take a moment to accept the situation you are in and look at the beauty of this frontier around you."

Rumpus bent over, cupping his hand and taking drinks of water while the lion started to hum again. "Leonidas," the creature announced. "Leonidas Reliance is my name, if you are wondering."

The thirsty rhino stopped drinking and made eye contact again. "Oh, I'm so sorry, my name is Rum—"

"Rumpus, yes I know! My friend here told me, and so did another old friend some time ago." The lion gestured upward over his shoulder. Rumpus followed the gesture of the happy lion, noticing a purple, twisted staff stuck firmly in the ground next to the rock. The bee eater, her rainbow feathers glimmering, sat on the crown of the walking stick. She leaned in toward Rumpus's horns with a focused stare and smile.

The little bird's intensity freaked Rumpus out a bit. They traded looks for another moment before the bee eater finally squeezed a long squint.

Rumpus copied her with a squint back, and this continued, as though the pair were having a conversation with their eyebrows.

"She was a friend of someone called El Vaquero years ago," the lion announced, breaking the game of eye gestures with his interruption. "You really remind her of her old buddy. I think she likes you, which is good. Having a bee eater as a friend is a good thing on this island."

Rumpus crinkled his eyebrows again at the bird, who again mimicked his expression. "I could use some friends," Rumpus admitted. "I'm not going to lie. I'm pretty scared."

"That's ok, Rumpus. There is nothing wrong with admitting a little fear," Leonidas comforted. "This place has beauty beyond measure, but there is plenty to be afraid of as well. Look at this stream you are drinking from and take a step over to the other side for me."

Breaking eye contact with his new feathered friend, Rumpus obliged Leonidas and crossed the creek to look at the two of them together. "Imagine you are standing on the stream of life and look in the direction it is flowing. You can see the twists and turns, and there are things you cannot see yet. It continues to bend back and forth; it gets smaller and wider. In some places it is crystal clear. Other places it is cloudy. There are areas that are calm and others that are troubled and rough. There are times where it overflows, and other times it looks dried up and waits for rain. This is your life, Rumpus, and all of us have a stream. As we head away from this spot into the Olive Jar Jungle, think about the blessing of being given this stream and the differences it has to offer you. Always be cognizant of the moment and what might be coming next. Enjoy the ride, my brother."

Rumpus was still looking downstream and soaking in these wise words. When Leonidas suddenly appeared on his left side, he was caught off guard.

"So, let's start following your stream, Rumpus!" The sage of a lion held his staff, the bee eater close to his head. In surprise, Rumpus looked back to the rock on the other side of the stream and saw the broken shackle on the ground. "I told you not to worry about it, my friend," Leonidas laughed, walking along the stream. "Try and keep up—and enjoy the view!"

And off the trio went, following the stream toward dense jungle in the distance. Once again, Rumpus wondered about the name El Vaquero.

Who was this guy?

CHAPTER 6

THE TELEPHONE GAME

On the plains far away, a young bee swished back and forth through the tufts of grass and bushes, making its way up the hill toward Vigil on the Plateau. He'd already visited the Baker, who was churning out cupcakes as fast as he could. The creatures in that area enjoyed the abundance of their favorite dish now wandering the land. It was rare to see so many at a time. Bakers were usually instructed to parse them out sparingly

to keep the balance of need, greed, and want that created a little bit of tension in the areas where they were assigned.

Through the tall grasses, the bee could see a lighthouse rising against the sky. When the messenger finally reached the shore, it buzzed up to the front door and grabbed the rope for a tug to alert the residents it was there. A gong echoed up the skyscraping lighthouse of a tower, and steps thundered down the stairs. A single rabbit guard posted at the top dozed in the warm day. It was his job to report on anything he saw that might be out of place. Management knew that the Resound Fields was a special place, the epicenter of where changes came from. It had been many years, though, and the post had become a source of jokes. Guards sent here were not so bright or were not useful enough,

people said. Management had become lazy, telling the guards to relax on their findings. Nothing in eight years had changed. Bored guards with nothing to do who didn't care too much got fat and enjoyed plenty of sleep.

This particular guard had missed everything that had happened when Sheol dropped off Rumpus. He'd swiveled the large spyglass into a horizontal position, using it for a large bed.

Now, however, the portly rabbit, wearing only half his uniform, opened the door. "Yes? Yes, what do you want?" he belched out. It had been weeks since he'd seen anyone, and he hoped it might be his cupcake delivery. They were getting further apart, which didn't match his lazy appetite. Raising his hand to shield himself from the setting suns, he squinted and saw the bee buzzing frantically.

"Telegenic Dome copies you, Vigil," a voice scratched back through the radio speaker, despite the guard's hopes that no one was going to answer.

His lip got closer to the mic, and he quietly spoke, "Sheol has returned and dropped off a visitor."

The following pause seemed to last a lifetime. It was broken with, "Can you repeat that, sir? Copy."

Buckets of sweat ran down his face as he repeated, "Sheol has returned and dropped off a visitor."

This time the pause was longer, which gave the rabbit time to flip the looking glass into the vertical position and scan the fields below, hoping to find something that would redeem his major screw up. There was nothing out there but an occasional bird and some Aqua Wisent grazing in the tall grass.

"We copy that, sir, and are checking the field cameras now. We will report our findings directly to the general and advise that you wait for further instructions. Did you see what the visitor looked like so we can identify it on our film?"

Before the rabbit had the time to crap his pants, the bee remarked, "It was a rhino, sir. It looked like a younger El Vaquero. He was met by Party Walrus and sent west to Port Croon." The rabbit backed away in shock and relief. Thank goodness the bee had accidently provided the info he needed! The fact that the visitor was a rhino felt significant even to a dunce like him.

The other listening station in the capital of Kaputar never responded. On the other side of that line was another rabbit not doing his job. There were a lot more distractions in the capital for a rabbit babysitting a transmission station, and on that side, there was no one in the room. He was down the hallway rolling dice with the other guards. That delay added a little bit of time to the life of the terrified tower guard.

Looking down at the ground, the Vigil guard said to the bee that saved his butt, "It looks like this may not be as bad as I thought. All we can do now is wait, I guess."

But when he looked up, the bee was gone. This bee was no dummy. He knew the guard's days were numbered and felt it wise to be as far away from the doomed soul as possible.

On the mini-island Amanuensis in the town of Lens was the Telegenic Dome. Most inhabitants of this island were pigs who took shifts monitoring the security screens that the hidden cameras around the island fed into. There were many things to watch and feeds to be concerned with.

Amanuensis

The island had been assigned their own personal Baker, and thus the surveillance team was very happy and plugged into the system. They didn't really enjoy supplying information on the creatures of Nisamehe, but the cupcake treats made doing the job a whole lot easier.

A group of them brought up the footage for the day in Resound Fields, and all crowded around the screen in anticipation of this historical event. The first camera they reviewed shared little that would help them. It started with a usually quiet day in the fields and a circular opening appearing in the sky. They could see the winds changing and lightning strikes from the edge of the circles hitting targets with small explosions. In a flash, one of the lightning strikes hit the camera, and the screen went dark.

Checking one camera after another, they realized all they had in the area was the same scene and ending, playing out from different vantage points. One of the pigs spoke up. "I'll radio General Von Hareliar and give him the news."

He grabbed the radio and called out, "Channel 2, do you have a copy?"

A gravel like voice returned instantly. "Go on 2."

With respect, the pig replied, "Sir, as you may have heard from Channel 6 already, there has been a sighting of significant importance. Sheol appeared and dropped off a visitor that looks like a rhino. He was intercepted by Party Walrus near his base and sent west to Port Croon. I'm afraid all the cameras in the fields were destroyed by the electrical storm, so we do not have visual confirmation beyond the report. We dispatched a team toward the fields to repair the cameras right away sir. Over."

The general sat at his paper-covered desk, plastered with tax reports and wanted posters, and stared at his plate of food. He preferred older ways of doing things and sat in the stone room by candlelight. Scratching the scar over one of his eyes and twisting one side of his burnt orange mustache, he leaned back in his chair and peered down the hallway. There he saw the guard that should have been monitoring Channel 6, rolling dice with a cupcake in one hand, laughing with the other guards. The general tipped his chair back to sitting position and grabbed his helmet to cover his soft brainpan. He picked up two scarred and war-torn billy clubs from the table, gripped one in each angry hand, and walked in the direction of his inadequate men.

CHAPTER 7

FRONDESCENCE AND THE SEEDS THEY NEED

Rumpus, Leonidas, and the bee eater headed into the dark Olive Jar Jungle. Leonidas hopped back and forth in front of Rumpus like a happy little kid exploring the landscape. The bee eater looked back on occasion with a smile on her beak. But despite his new friends, a part of Rumpus remained worried. When he considered all the bizarre stuff that had happened—was following a naked lion with a headband and a bee eater something he should really be doing? Was this the new norm? What options did he really have?

At least talking to Leonidas gave him some peace, and he was moving forward on the stream of life, as the lion so colorfully described it. Leonidas was right. If this was a place that he was destined to come to, then he should look around and enjoy it. Thinking back on where he was and his mental state back home, there was something exciting about the difference in his life. His senses were on overload with all the different creatures, the vibrant colors, and even the occasional remnants of graffiti providing an interesting twist, considering the contrast. Some of the paint spelled out names he had seen in the natural world. It gave him comfort to have something he loved from home also in this place, but also raised some questions with the overlap.

Breathing and taking it all in, he started to notice that it was getting darker. The fingers of the forest treetops bowed toward him like a crashing wave, with beams of light struggling to break through the holes in the lush canopy of olive-colored foliage. He noticed the bark of the trees, the strange bushes, and even the dirt were all shades of olive, ranging from drab to saturated. It was beautiful, and even the water changed from a crystal blue to a translucent green under the shadows of the treetops.

Leonidas pushed ahead through some high bushes, and Rumpus could only see the top of his head and the bobbing walking stick with the bee eater perched on top. Rumpus took a deep breath and said, "Well, here goes nothing. Stream of life and all that good stuff."

A shout came from over the bushes. "Come on, Rumpus! Let's stick together. Come on in, the water is fine!"

The big rhino pushed the bushes aside and ventured into the lush jungle. Soon, he came out into a clearing, and Leonidas was farther down into a ravine. It was amazing. Every direction this curious rhino looked, he saw small, flying, olive-colored creatures with glowing parts dancing through the air and pollinating the flowers and vegetation. Lights flashed on and off as tiny, lightning-like bugs revealed themselves and disappeared. Waves of seeds floated down with feather-like wings, lodging themselves into the ground, landing on Rumpus's clothes. The small creatures illuminated every move; he looked down at his arms to see the funny little bugs looking up at him and smiling.

"Come on, buddy! I found us a ride!" the lion sage shouted out.

Rumpus looked over to see Leonidas mounting a strange creature, like he was getting onto a horse. The creature had two large, banded, strong elephantine legs and a fat, crocodile-like body with the end of its tail glowing like a light up bulb. Its head was like a camel with catfish whiskers and skinny, bunny-like ears. Rumpus was pleased to realize he was no longer as shocked by encountering a new, strange creature.

"What is it?" Rumpus shouted out.

"An Olivelapod!" Leonidas laughed. "Hop aboard!"

Rumpus sidled up to the Olivelapod, looking for a way to climb on this majestic creature. "Grab on to his neck, go on!" the comical old lion urged. "They are really strong and love it when they have a rider!"

The Olivelapod bobbled back and forth. Rumpus climbed onto a rock to grab its neck, then hurled his body up onto its back. The creature's catfish like whiskers started to grow, making their way back to Rumpus's hands until he was holding them like reins.

"Well look who got the hang of it all the sudden!" Leonidas cheered. "Hold on tight to those reins and imagine where you want to go. It'll all fall into place. May I suggest imagining yourself following me, since I know where we are going? Off to the Frondescence!"

Leonidas took off down the ravine, with the Olivelapod bouncing down the path next to the stream. Rumpus squeezed his mount's tentacles and imagined himself following Leonidas. Off they bounded, matching the exact places the rider and steed were taking in front of him.

The sweet air swam over his wrinkled, brick-like muzzle, horns, and ears as they bounced through the forest. It was thrilling, and Rumpus was starting to enjoy himself. They started to slow, and Rumpus pulled up next to Leonidas on his ride. The old lion was gazing up at a bunch of large trees where pinecone-like giant mud houses and buildings swayed among the branches, rope bridges

Olive Jar Jungle

connecting them. All kinds of creatures worked and went about their daily lives. Some looked like animals Rumpus knew from his own world, and others reminded him of the aliens from the *Star Wars* movie cantina. Above them, a humming creature with four eyes and a frog face hummed as she beat a rug. A rabbit walked by with a basket of what looked like glowing fruits or vegetables loaded on his back. At the base of the trees stood a whole market where walk up mini ramen spots sold the most delicious smelling food Rumpus had ever smelled.

"You hungry?" he heard as Leonidas dismounted his ride and smacked it on the butt to release it. "I would let those whiskers go before you go for a ride back into the forest."

Letting go instantly, Rumpus started his dismount as the Olivelapod took off running. Rumpus toppled down onto his backside.

"Haha, stop goofing around!" Leonidas said, offering Rumpus a hand. "Let's get some ramen. It's time we meet Madam FoSho. She always tells the best stories and revelations."

A rhino, a lion, and a bee-eating bird all took a seat at a bar. It sounded like the beginning of a weird joke, and Rumpus had to admit they looked funny. He and Leonidas took a seat at the FoSho Flavororium, a four-seat walk-up ramen spot with a giant mushroom cap overhang, while the bee eater flew up to a low branch nearby.

"What do you handsome fellas fancy today?" a portly creature with four eyes asked, batting green glitter eyelids at them. Her tattoo-covered arm rested on the counter. The ink began at her wrist as a seed and showed steps of growth going up her arm until it was an illuminated lightbulb on her shoulder. "My eyes are up here, honey," she chuckled as she looked at Rumpus.

"He'll take the shotake wildshroom ramen with leaf nuts, Madam FoSho, and I'll take the special," Leonidas told the hostess, and she paused with a mischievous smile.

"Coming right up, gentlemen," she said, dropping a seed on the counter in front of Rumpus and turning around to prepare their food.

Out of the corner of her eye, Madam FoSho noticed Rumpus looking at a cage full of cupcakes that all seemed to be watching them. "You want one of those cupcakes, sweetness?" she said with a smile. Leonidas put his hand on Rumpus's wrist and squeezed.

Rumpus answered softly, "No, ma'am."

"Ma'am!" she snorted and turned around. "Now I haven't been called a ma'am for some time—in fact, I never heard the term until El Vaquero started eating here. You don't want none of those dirty cakes anyway. Good for you, sugar horns."

Rumpus looked down, and the seed now had a sprout sticking out of it.

"Yeees sir-ee, been a minute since I've been called something that fancy. In fact, the last time I made shotake wildshroom ramen was for him," she explained as she put a gigantic bowl of ramen in front of the rhino and flicked the seed with her chubby pinky finger, making it spin and the seedling grow a little taller.

She reminded him of his grandma, Rumpus realized: she was kind of feisty and talked with sass and warmth. Madam FoSho had turned back around to work on Leonidas's bowl, barking back at the lion, "You want extra spice leaves or what, ya old goat?"

The lion laughed. "You ask every time…"

But before he could finish Madam FoSho cut him off. "You shut your mouth, ya kook. You know I ask because of how rare they are. In fact, the guy who always sat next to you with horns like his always got a couple leaves in his bowl too." She turned to Rumpus as the rhino was mid-slurp. "You want a couple in yours?"

Rumpus looked at his new lion friend and got a nod back. "Yes, ma'am," he answered, and a hand dropped in two spice leaves, then pointed to the seed on the table, now a full sprout with a bulb on top and root legs on the countertop. Rumpus paused and examined the seedling. What was making it grow right there on the table, and why did she put it there?

They sat and ate in silence while Madam FoSho put things back in their places. He savored every bite and occasionally looked around at other shops, where fantastic animals and creatures ate and traded in the marketplace.

"You know, only one other person ever finished that bowl of ramen, and he had horns just like you," Madam FoSho said casually. "A little more weathered, but just like you."

"He would hardly ever talk when eating, either," chimed in Leonidas.

"A'right, a'right…this mention of this El Vaquero is almost starting to get a little annoying," Rumpus grumbled. "The weird creature when I got spit out by a whale, the drunk walrus telling me to go to Limerick Cove, cupcakes, a bee eater who thinks I look like him…this is all getting to be too much!"

Before he could go any further, a voice to his right broke his rant. "And what is wrong with being compared to the greatest being to ever visit our island?"

Rumpus paused; he hadn't even realized anyone else was eating there. He looked to his right, and there was the creature he'd met right after being spit out of the whale. "I never got to give you my name. I'm Dizzie Ataxicmax, more commonly known as DJ OMC. I think you might need to relax and listen to Madam FoSho for a minute."

The ninja-like pop-up style of the island's inhabitants was becoming all too common, so Rumpus closed his mouth and looked straight ahead. Madam FoSho was looking back with him with loving eyes. "You finished, honey? I know you were not raised to talk like that to people trying to get you help."

"Yes, ma'am," he answered sheepishly.

Putting three arms on her hips, she pointed down to the seed pod on the counter; Rumpus followed her direction to glance back down at the plant growing next to him. The bulb on the top of the stalk was glowing.

"Baby, he loved you so much," she said quietly. "Have you ever stopped to think about what the name El Vaquero means?"

Leonidas spoke up. "I don't even remember what it means!"

"Shuuuut it, ya old kook," Madam FoSho said, one of her hands pointing at the lion's nose. "I'm getting there." She turned back to Rumpus. "It means 'The Cowboy,'" she explained quietly as the bulb dislodged from the stem and floated up, emanating light. "He loved you very much and often said you would be the only other one to finish this bowl."

Rumpus was fixated on the bulb's movement as it glowed. He heard what she said and was just starting to process the words "he loved you" when

it popped, and he shuddered. The light illuminated a photo on the back wall. Staring for a minute in disbelief, he found himself staring at a picture of his grandfather. "He loved you so much and finished his bowl just to make the wall of fame, just so you would find it," she continued. "Every time he ate here, he would laugh and say that he knew that you would make your way to the greatest ramen spot on the island."

Tears rolled down the tough rhino skin of Rumpus's cheeks. He'd had a feeling all this time that they might be talking about his grandpa. In fact, he hoped that was the case, but everyone seemed to have so much admiration for him that he wasn't sure. Grandpa Duncan was so quiet, it was more likely that no one would notice him. He'd liked it that way back home. Why would so many people admire him here? He just wasn't that guy — the greatest being that ever visited the island, as he'd just been described. But the picture on the wall was him, and he was the greatest to Rumpus! What happened to gain him that kind of fame? Grandpa always did say that he was born in the wrong era and that he would have been a cowboy out on the plains, exploring and drawing in his sketchbook.

"Baby? Baby, look at me. You OK? I know this is a lot," Madam FoSho said as she put her hand on his.

Another hand came down on his left shoulder.

"We haven't seen him for a while, but that doesn't mean he isn't on the island somewhere. Maybe we can find him together," Leonidas offered with a gentle smile. "What would really help is if we could find his field guide. There are so many answers in there from the things he recorded. He said it had a special power running through it. That book might hold the clues to where he could be."

Rumpus wiped his eyes and looked over at the lion. "A field guide?"

Leonidas leaned back in his chair and relaxed. "That's what he used to call it. He drew and wrote notes on everything he saw. The things he figured out in that book and shared freed a lot of us from what is out there. Vaquero is a hero to us."

Rumpus looking back at the picture, noticing a large plunger above the frame mounted to the wall. "So where is his field guide, and what's up with the plunger mounted over his picture?" he asked.

Madam FoSho was already reaching for it, pulling it off the wall. She handed it over to Rumpus. "This was his favorite weapon."

Rumpus couldn't help but chuckle. "A plunger? He always liked the weirdest things."

"Well, he never set out to kill, but found a way to do some amazing things with that. He always laughed and said he would unclog their ears, hearts, or minds, but he had no problem defending himself to the fullest." Madam FoSho pointed to the name burned into the wooden handle: "One TON."

Rumpus gripped it like he was giving his grandpa a hug. "I need to find that field guide as soon as possible. Why didn't you tell me sooner?"

Leonidas shrugged. "We had to be sure who you were. We haven't seen Vaquero in a year or so. It's hard to know who to trust."

A scream behind interrupted the story. "STOP! You there! How did you get off your chain? Stop in the name of Mr. Omega."

Two rabbits charged toward them. The shorter of the two wore a military uniform and swung a small club; the other was a huge rabbit goon in a uniform clearly too small for him, with his belly jiggling out of his rolled-up shirt. His bulky arm swung his club above his head, making it look like a pencil in his catcher's mitt of a hand. Rumpus scrambled off of his stool, pushing Leonidas behind him just as the larger of the two rabbits punched him straight in the face. Rumpus stumbled backward, reaching to catch himself on the countertop. He bumped into the plunger, and it rolled off the bar into

his hand. Rumpus looked at his new weapon as Leonidas and DJ OMC wrestled the two rabbits next to him. Rumpus gripped the handle and sprung to his feet, swinging with an uppercut, connecting the plunger to the jaw of the large rabbit. The goon's jaw stretched up past his face at least a foot before the rest of his body realized

it was supposed to be traveling upward, and his feet left the ground as he flew through the air before landing flat on his back on the bar. Madam FoSho grabbed a cupcake out of the cage and shoved it into the goon's mouth, grabbing his jaw and vigorously making his jaw chew, then stroking his throat, to make him swallow. The rabbit slid off the bar in a daze.

The smaller rabbit stopped punching on DJ OMC and looked at Rumpus in shock. "Who are you? We haven't seen you on the…"

Just then, Leonidas smashed a stool on the guard's head and dragged the dazed rabbit over to the bar for a cupcake that would make him forget anything that happened.

"Run, Rumpus...RUN!" Leonidas ordered. "We will catch up with you. Find an Olivelapod and think about a ring of thorns. It will know where to go. We will catch up to you! Hurry and go!"

Rumpus started to run but realized he'd dropped his only connection to his grandpa. He scrambled back for his new weapon, One TON.

"I said run, Rumpus!" screamed Leonidas as DJ OMC stuffed a cupcake down the small rabbit's gullet and Madam FoSho tied up the larger one. Rumpus hauled butt through the town, once bumping into a strange slug-like creature with laundry on her head and knocking her silky clothes to the ground, before he found an Olivelapod. Rumpus climbed up on the creature's back, grabbing its whiskers as he closed his eyes. He imagined a large ring of thorns. Suddenly the Olivelapod was off and running, and the town of Frondescene disappeared in the distance. Rumpus was alone again, hurtling his way down a path to yet another new location. He only hoped that he would learn more about where his grandpa had gone.

CHAPTER 8

A THORN IN HIS SIDE

Rumpus and his new trusty steed broke through the edge of the jungle and came out onto a grass clearing where he could see the ocean. His ride started to slow, trotting up to a giant wall of thorns. Looking back and forth, Rumpus noticed a curve in the wall and picked a direction to see if his answers were around the corner.

After riding for a minute with the ocean on his side, he found himself facing inland again, with the edge of the jungle visible in the distance. "Did I just go around this thing in a big circle?" he wondered aloud. He climbed down from the Olivelapod to inspect the wall of thorns. Letting go of the whisker still in his hand, he carefully rested his hands on the large crusty vines.

His not-so-trusty steed took that opportunity to run off.

"Nooooo!" Rumpus yelled out, reaching toward the already too-far-off Olivelapod. His shoulders and arms dropped as he slumped over. "No" he whispered.

Residents of the island knew what Rumpus didn't: Olivelapods roam in packs. When a rider lets go of their whiskers, they run back to rejoin that pack. The creature was only doing what was natural to it, but even had he known, it wouldn't have made Rumpus feel any better.

The rhino turned his attention back to the wall of thorns. Why had Leonidas sent him to this location? "There has got to be something on the other side of this wall," he muttered.

Rumpus walked around the circle, looking closely for something he could have missed. Nothing on this island seemed to be his version of normal anyway, so he needed to look for something that didn't make sense to him. At least it was a start. The thorns and woody vines were thick and braided so tightly that he couldn't see through. Finally, he came to an area that looked dented in. Rumpus paused. The vines were thinner, so he grabbed a couple, pulling and pushing on them until they finally revealed some light on the other side.

Rumpus leaned in to peer through a space about half the size of his fist. "Ouch!" He pulled back out, looking down at his side. His curiosity had made him forget about the thorns; one had poked his side hard enough to tear his sweatshirt and draw blood. With care, Rumpus tried again, poking his head in for a better look. Having eyes more on the side of his head made some things easier and others harder. This was harder. He had to wedge his head to the side and push some thorns into his face to get a better look. He could finally see inside the ring.

The first thing he noticed were the lush green grass and thousands of wildflowers of species he had never seen before. They looked like dollops of pearlescent paint and shimmered in the two suns. Funny little bugs were flying around, and it almost seemed like a different shade of sunlight came just into this area. Rumpus started to look farther when he noticed something very familiar to him, but it was still rare even in his world. Vines worked their way from a dark base up to a rounded metal box. It was an old payphone! A wire rose out of the back, but about twenty feet up into the air, it just disappeared. What in the world was a payphone doing out in the middle of nowhere and on this island?

A noise above his head made Rumpus jerk his head out of the thorns. He took a couple scratches deep into his face. His hand on his cheek, he squinted his eyes and looked upward to the top of the thorn covered wall. It was the bee eater! He quickly turned around to see if his friends had finally shown up, but no, he was still alone—at least in the sense of someone who would talk back.

"Where are the guys?" he asked the bee eater. His bird friend just looked at him, fluffed up, and started cleaning her feathers. Rumpus followed the bird's gaze out to the ocean, but there was nothing there. The sun was setting, and Rumpus sat down for a minute, thinking maybe the others would be there soon. He fell asleep for a little bit with his watcher perched over him. Hours had passed when he was woken by a branch falling at his feet. His bird buddy was pulling on old branches of the vine and breaking off pieces, dropping them in a pile near Rumpus's feet.

"What's going on? What are you doing?" Rumpus asked, but as usual there was no answer. The sun was low on the horizon when the bird dropped one more branch and flew straight up into the air, doing a backward flip into the ring.

Everything went silent for Rumpus.

"Hello?" he called out. The two suns were sinking below the water when Rumpus noticed shapes coming out of the ocean. They were shadows with the light at their backs, and they walked like crocodiles. Rumpus could hear grunts and snarls surrounding him. Dark purple shadows moved toward him, their eyes winking on with a glow, like the scheduled timing of streetlights in the city. Rumpus scrambled to his feet, ready to run, when the bee eater landed next to him with a bug creature in her mouth. The bird shoved it into the pile of sticks and branches, then took the end of her beak and smacked the bug on the head several times. The little guy became so frustrated that it started to glow, and then burst into a little flame, setting the dried-out branches ablaze.

The fire blossomed into a huge illuminating flower, revealing shadows right on top of them, light-illuminated rows of eyes and teeth in every direction. The light scared the creatures back, though, and Rumpus could finally see what they were. He'd been right: they were very crocodile-like. Their heads were longer than their bodies, with eyes bulging out like old lightbulbs and rows of pink, luminescent teeth. Their midsections were half the length of their heads, with six legs, webbed feet with claws, and long tails with flat, whale-like flukes on the end. Their fear of the light made Rumpus

suspect they were nocturnal. He stripped onto the dry branches of the wall, stripping off segments to make the fire bigger and drive the creatures farther back. As the fire grew, the sea creatures pushed on each other to get away, starting to fight with each other in a hunger fever.

"Well, I guess all we gotta do is keep this up all night, huh?" groaned Rumpus as he threw on another branch. He looked back at where the fire almost touched the wall of thorns, then down the wall beyond, considering the possibility of running back to the jungle. There were no streetlights here, though, and total darkness was mere steps away. Who knew what was waiting out there, or how far the creatures would chase them?

Hours passed. Rumpus and the bee eater held strong, and the fire had grown. Many of the creatures had left to look for other food, with only a couple stragglers still watching the new friendship being literally forged in fire. Rumpus was dry and exhausted. He reached back behind him to break off another piece of the large vines when he noticed that the fire was starting to dry out the wall, too. It was getting easier to break pieces off. He crouched down and started yanking away branches; they broke easily, revealing a hole. Frantically he worked to enlarge the hole, ignoring the thorns and tossing the brush behind him. He even started digging with his bare hands to make a small tunnel. His hand popped through the other side, which gave him cause to work harder.

He broke and tore and threw. When he glanced behind him, he noticed the fire was a little smaller. "Please throw the scrap on the fire!" he cried out to the bee eater, then turned his attention back to the escape hatch he was working on. The bee eater quickly picked up the sticks and flew above the fire, strategically dropping them in the right places, but they were running out of fuel with Rumpus so focused on digging.

"I can get myself in! I can get myself in!" Rumpus cried out, pushing his backpack through the other side and turning himself onto his back to squeeze through the small tunnel he had made. The fire was dying, and Rumpus locked eyes with one of the two sea monsters waiting for their barbecue. He dug his heels into the ground and pushed into the tunnel, wiggling his stocky body. The fire was almost out, and Rumpus could hear the fervor of his hunters' excitement. The ground shook, and Rumpus realized the creatures had overcome the fear of the fire and were charging at him—

He pulled his last leg through the hole, and a crunch resonated from on the outside wall, followed by the squeals of an unlucky creature hitting the thorns. Rumpus had made it to a safe space.

It was still so dark he could barely see anything around him. He couldn't see the phone booth in the center and was hesitant to move from his spot, so he sat back down and clutched his bag. The occasional lightning bug flashed, and Rumpus heard the sea creatures finally get bored and head back into the darkness to eat before sunrise.

His head drooped as his adrenaline wore off. Sitting there with his legs pulled up to his chest, he started to rest his head on his knees and close his eyes when the bee eater landed on the top of his backpack. Since it was dark and he was scared, his first instinct was to wave his hands like a crazy person. The bird flew up into the air, and the flash of a couple lightning bugs revealed Rumpus's feathered partner.

"I'm sorry…I'm sorry," he said, laying on his side in a fetal position. The bee eater landed back on Rumpus's shoulder and pressed her head onto Rumpus's cheek in comfort. Her beak made its way up to his ear, and the way her breath flowed through her beak almost sounded like the word "Agape."

"Is that your name?" Rumpus murmured as he drifted off. The bird didn't answer, but a series of taps on Rumpus's shoulder gave him the answer he needed. They fell asleep in peace.

CHAPTER 9

BREAK OF DAWN

Rumpus and Agape slept all night like a couple of rocks piled on top of each other. As the sun broke over the horizon, a soft breeze blew through the grass, sending a sweet smell to dance around Rumpus. As the rhino's heavy eyelids started to open, he heard Agape land next to him. His feathered friend had dropped off some fruit and rolled what looked like an apple toward him, though the bird herself chomped on berries. Rumpus sat up and took a bite, then noticed the phone booth again. He stood up and dusted himself off, reaching down put to his backpack back on. Agape landed on his shoulder and nudged him, letting him know that he should walk toward the phone booth.

"Well, that was an adventure," Rumpus said, glancing at the bird. "Last night was crazy. Your name is Agape, right?" he asked. Everything had been so overwhelming the night before, he wasn't sure if he remembered it correctly.

His new buddy started nudging him on the cheek again, cooing, bringing a smile to Rumpus's face. "Did you know my grandpa? Were you friends with him too?"

Agape flew up into the air tucking, her wings and spinning in the air in joy before landing back on Rumpus's shoulder, grinding her head into the rhino's cheek. "Haha, I'll take that as a yes!"

Rumpus remembered the payphone in the center of the ring of thorns, covered in vines, stickers, and marker tags. "I wonder if this will allow me to call home," Rumpus mused. "Who would I call, anyway? And what would they do to help? Maybe I could at least tell Mom and Dad what happened to Grandpa, and that I am now in this place."

Agape left his shoulder and flew ahead while Rumpus walked to the booth. Just as Agape started to land on top of it, the phone rang. Rumpus paused and stared at the phone for the first three rings. He'd never thought about someone calling in. He snapped himself out of his hesitation and ran to the old phone booth. Reaching for the phone, he paused one more time, closed his eyes, and blew out a breath. His hand landed on the receiver and slowly pulled it up to his ear.

"Ahh...hel...hello?" he said timidly.

A scratchy voice on the other end answered back, sounding like one of those old-time New York female operators like he'd seen in the movies. "Hello there, Rumpus. We have been waiting for you. Better late than never. Please hold while we connect you to Upper Management."

A series of clicks preceded another phone ringing on another side. "Upper Management's office, executive assistant Dawn speaking."

Rumpus cleared his throat and answered. "This is Rumpus—"

Before he could get any further, the voice interrupted him with excitement. "Ahhhh, Mr. Rumpus! We have been patiently waiting for you. How was your first night on the island?"

Looking up at Agape on top of the phone booth, Rumpus answered in confusion. "It was ok, if you like almost getting yourself eaten by some sort of sea monsters…"

Not even phased by the statement, the assistant on the other end continued, "Well that is great to hear! We have been excited for you to get here and enjoy yourself. One of our best operatives, Agape, has already found you and will be your counsel. Although she doesn't talk much, you are in good feathers! We understand that you have a lot of questions, but first we need to get you your grandpa's field guide. Many of those questions will have the answers there! So sit back and relax, and enjoy the ride on this stream we called life. We are sending one of our helpers to fly you to your next destination." She took a breath, and when she continued, he could hear the smile in her voice. "It's great to hear a voice, because we haven't had any calls in years. There are other phones on the island, so we will hopefully talk again soon. Thank you for the call, and we will be in touch. Have a great day!"

Just like that, the call ended.

DAWN...

On the other end, Dawn hung up the phone and signaled with her hand to have someone come up to her desk. Dawn had been working there for longer than anyone had ever known. She was puffy and soft and made of clouds. She emanated rays of sunshine when she was happy and radiated storm when having a bad day. She wasn't a complicated lady, but she was incredibly smart and loyal. Her desk didn't have much on it, just a large, red landline phone next to a Rolodex she rarely needed. A stack of yellow Post-it notes stood near two pens, one blue and one red. No one but Dawn knew if there was a reason for the two colors.

Dawn had a foolproof system for getting things done. On the left side of her desk was a small laptop and two delicate figurines of French bulldog puppies playing. That was all she needed to get things done for Upper Management.

Across her desk, a unique creature arrived to her summons. She looked a bit like a griffin. Her name was Sunny, and she had a bird's head, a fat cheetah's body, and a set of eagle's wings on her back.

"He was late, but he finally made it to the checkpoint," Dawn reported. "It's time to go pick him up and drop him off at the town of Mynewsha in the Arion Ater Mountains. We need to get this show on the road." She glanced up at Sunny with a serious expression. "Don't forget to stay out of range of the cameras near the Resound Fields." Then the sunshine returned to her cheeks. "Oh, he might even make it there in time for the Running of the Hamsters! Please report back once you have dropped him off so I can let Upper Management know. Have a safe trip!"

As Dawn completed her instructions, she went straight back to answering messages on her computer. Sunny looked toward the Upper Management door down the hall a hundred yards away, looked back at the door across from Dawn's desk, and trotted off on her mission with a happy bounce. Outside Dawn's door in the hallway was a platform, and Sunny bounded over, jumping into its ring. BLIP! Sunny shrank to the size of a peanut and disappeared.

High in the sky above the lower part of the island, a peanut appeared and—BLIP!—Sunny dove toward the ring of thorns she could see a mile down. As she picked up speed, the sound was reminiscent of the noise old bomber planes made when dropping bombs.

Down below, Rumpus was still looking around and talking to Agape. "So what are we supposed to do now? What did she mean by flying me to my next destination?"

He ambled toward the bird on top of the phone booth until he noticed the noise of a falling bomb. The suns were behind Sunny, and Rumpus couldn't make out any details of the growing dot in the sky. He started to worry. It looked like it was coming straight at him!

With a glance at Agape, who lifted off to fly up and circle overhead, Rumpus jogged away from the phone booth, toward the hole he had dug the previous night. The bomber sound grew louder, and Rumpus picked up the pace as he realized that the vines had grown back. He turned to the left, running alongside the inside wall of the thorns and hoping that whatever was coming down would strike a different location than his own. Rumpus still couldn't see anything, so he decided staying in motion would be safest. The noise sounded right on top of him, and he saw Agape zoom toward the center of the ring. Agape had always had a way of knowing what to do, so Rumpus turned and ran as fast as he could after the bird. The sound surrounded them, and Rumpus was so scared he could hardly breathe…

A pair of claws grabbed his shoulders. Rumpus was propelled forward, his feet dragging on the grass before leaving the ground. Up and up he soared, out of the ring of thorns and toward the ocean. Rumpus screamed in terror, clutching his hands over his eyes. As they started to turn, Rumpus finally realized that he wasn't going to fall. They were turning back toward land and flying over the ring of thorns. To his right, Agape soared on the wind current and gave Rumpus a little wink, like everything was going to be OK. Glancing above his head, Rumpus could see a long neck with cheetah spots and a hawk's head, smiling. Massive iridescent wings swooshed on each side of him as the Olive Jar Jungle passed under his dangling feet.

The large griffin twisted her neck so he could see Rumpus. "Hey there, buddy!" she said in a melodic baritone voice, while Rumpus's face reflected in her giant eyeball. Rumpus was absurdly reminded of Barry White. "Are you ready to find that field guide?" the griffin asked while she straightened her head back in the direction they were flying.

"Where are we going?" Rumpus yelled back, looking down at the dense jungle speeding under his feet.

"My name is Sunny! Thanks for asking!" the griffin answered with a laugh.

Rumpus was a little ashamed he hadn't thought to ask. He looked over at Agape and saw the bird snicker. "I'm sorry! Nice to meet you, Sunny," Rumpus backtracked. "My name is—"

Sunny burst out, "The Mighty, Mighty Ruuumpus!"

"No, just Rumpus," the rhino laughed, squirming a little from the way the griffin's talon dug into his shoulders and armpits. "I'm not going to lie, Sunny, this is starting to get a little sore."

Sunny looked back down at Rumpus. "We can take care of that. All we've got to do is get you up onto my back, if you are willing to ride the rest of the way."

Rumpus started to answer, "That would be great, let's just laaaAAAAAAAaaaand—"

The goofy griffin had stopped in midair, swinging her front arms to send a full-size rhino flying and flipping in the air, over her head. Rumpus landed on her back. Shaking, the rhino clung to her neck.

"Not really what I had in mind, Sunny," he gasped.

Sunny swished back and forth, laughing. "Rumpus, we just don't have time to waste on landing, and this isn't the place to do it. We're coming up on the edge of the Resound Fields, and we need to climb now. They have cameras around the perimeter, and we need to stay out of sight. Besides, once we get over the tops of that mountain ridge on the left, the town isn't far down the other side."

The three of them started to climb and bank to the left to turn toward the mountains. Rumpus looked off to the right past Agape and could barely make out the pond where he had met Party Walrus. The land just kept going; the island was so much bigger than he imagined. Purple rocks passed beneath them until they formed into a large mass, then turned into a mountain range. So many shades of purple shimmered in the morning sun, and their shadow danced over the rocks dropping in and out of crevices. They climbed up the cliffs, and the air started to get colder and crisp.

"I suggest holding on tight, buddy," Sunny called. "Grab that neck tighter—NOW!"

Rumpus tightened his grip just as Sunny broke the top of the mountain, shot up, and stopped flapping his wings. Leaning to the right and tucking her wings in, they barrel rolled together. After two spins, her wings shot back out, pausing and catching the wind like two parachutes, slowing them down as they started to coast down the other side of the mountain.

"There it is, Rumpus!" Sunny announced. "The town of Mynusha, where we are going to find that field guide of your grandpa's."

Rumpus smiled. "How do you know it's in the town?"

"That's the last place that anyone saw it," Sunny explained. "Since then, many have tried but no one has ever found it. I think it's because it has been waiting for you." Sunny tipped to the left, turning to give Rumpus a better view. "Judging from what I can see in the distance," the griffin continued, "it looks like we are getting there just in time for the Running of the Hamsters, and you are in for a real treat!"

Rumpus was starting to make out the shape of the cute little town. It was tucked into the mountainside, and Rumpus could see a large main town circle with a cobblestone road traveling up the mountain.

Stacked dome buildings in different colors lined the sides of the main path, and small, finger-like roads led to smaller houses. Another road headed down the mountain in a winding snake line, with more domes lining the descent. The buildings eventually stopped, and the road kept going down the mountainside and into the valley below. Rumpus had never seen anything like it, and he loved it. His attention turned toward a crowd of inhabitants gathering in the town circle, and he could hear a marching band playing as citizens danced around them in the street.

Sunny came in for a landing right in the middle of the square, but no one paid the three new arrivals any mind; they were all pumped up for the annual Running of the Hamsters. Creatures from all over the island came to see it each year, making it the town's biggest annual tourist pull.

Rumpus climbed down from Sunny, and Agape landed on one of the building ledges. A drunken rabbit with a half-eaten cupcake in his hand grabbed Rumpus's arm, chanting, "Hamsta! Hamsta! Hamsta!" He bobbed his head, trying to get Rumpus to chant with him, but when he didn't get what he wanted, he let go, spinning around in delight and chanting as he danced away.

As Rumpus looked around, he saw creatures of all types wearing red sashes on their waists. Others had signs with hamsters painted on them. Some even wore hamster suits and carried balloons shaped like hamsters. Everywhere Rumpus looked, vendors sold goods to creatures in pure bliss.

Sunny trotted over to snap Rumpus out of his crowd-watching daze. "Isn't this great!" the griffin chuckled. "Follow me. I'll take you to my favorite spot to watch the run!"

CHAPTER 10

RUN, HAMSTER RUN!

Sunny flew up and grabbed Rumpus again by the shoulders, gliding over to a large, twisted tree to one side of the large town circle. Rumpus grabbed onto a large branch and took a seat. Sunny landed next to him on the larger branch below. The dazed rhino could see the whole circle, and everything up to the road to his left. Slightly behind him to the right, he noticed the road winding back and forth down the mountainside. The energy in the air was electric, and Rumpus couldn't help but get excited when he saw all the happy folks of Mynusha and their visitors. Sunny looked up to him from the lower branch. "You are in for a real treat, Rumpus. This is one of the biggest events of the year on the island."

Rumpus couldn't help but ask, "What in the world am I looking at here?"

The griffin answered in pure excitement, "I haven't seen this in years! Creatures from all over the island show up and line up for a run, wearing those red sashes. Then members of the town line up with a hundred hamster cages, releasing them. The runners see how far they can get down the road before jumping off on the sides. The last runner remaining who gets the farthest wins a year's supply of cupcakes. Now, personally, I don't eat cupcakes, but the sport of it all is like nothing you have ever seen!"

Rumpus looked around and laughed. "Hamsters chasing people? This is what they call sport here?"

The music stopped, and a hush fell over the town. A pudgy little guy with two heads wearing a fancy suit and top hats walked out into the square. A worm with a party hat on his head pulled a wheeled wooden crate next to him. They stopped in unison, and the two-headed worm stepped up onto the crate, pulling out a bullhorn hanging from a strap at his side. The two heads bumped each other, each trying to be the first one to talk, until the head with a mustache won. "Hello, my fellow Mynushans and visitors from all over Nisamehe Island!"

The band started instantly rocking out as the people cheered. The host's hand went back up in the air, cutting the whole crowd right back to silence. "As Mayor of Mynusha, I am proud to commence the three hundred and twenty-first annual RUNNING OF THE HAMSTERS!"

The line of drummers started a beat back up, with the crowd bobbing in unison again, until the mayor's hand raised back up. "Since you're not here to listen to me, I'm not going to hold this event up anymore." He turned behind him, asking ceremoniously, "Are the cage agents ready to release those wild and vicious hamsters?!"

All attention turned to a hundred cages, where ten handlers held ropes connected to pulley systems on the doors. A little frog in a jumpsuit ran out, pointed an oversized flare gun into the air, and pulled the trigger. A small pop of light shot out and arced at only four feet, giving a wimpy flash and a pop.

A member of the crowd shouted from the back: "FAIL! You had one job!"

The frog drooped his shoulders and walked back behind the cages. The crowd's attention shifted back to the mayor, now on the side of the circle and back up on the box. He had his airhorn in one hand and the bullhorn up to the head with no mustache. "I guess that means they are ready! Let's get this party started!" And the mayor blasted the airhorn up towards the sky.

The Running of the Hamsters had been a time-honored tradition in the town of Mynusha for hundreds of years, but not everyone loved it like the other creatures of the island. Some hamsters really hated it. One such hamster was old Jebadiya Roundcheeks. He had participated as a runner for several years, and when he retired, his son Ronald took over. Every year the inhabitants started the run and taunted the hamsters as they frolicked past. But were they brave enough to do a run with a creature that could actually hurt them? No! Over the years, the irony of the whole event became the town's favorite joke—but not everyone involved was laughing. Most of the hamsters didn't care, but a few here and there joined the HRR—also known as the Hamster Run Resistance—and old Jebadiya was the president. He hated how the townspeople would put on the red sashes and act like they were running from fierce creatures, then point and laugh at the cute hamsters trying to bite their ankles. Jebadiya already knew he was small, but the villagers making them *feel* so small really burned him up. So, he came up with a plan to get them all back.

Jebadiya remembered chasing the rabbit guard in his last race. His target turned around and pointed at him, laughing, while the little hamster charged. He leapt into the air to try and land on his foot to bite him, but instead, a swift kick launched him across the road and into a haystack.

Jebadiya had since discovered a flower up in the mountain that, when crushed and mixed with the honey from the bees in the Floating Flotian Islands and some Berslag cinnamon, would make things grow. He escaped the town and moved farther up the mountain into one of the caves, where he took care of his two grandsons, Jason and Don. Every day for two years, he fed them some of a mixture he called "The Getback Juice," showing them movie reels of Hamster Runs of the past on the walls of his cave. He carefully pointed out when the inhabitants insulted the hamsters, pausing the film and pointing out shop owners and townspeople he thought were particularly cruel. Jason and Don were good boys, and over two years' time they had grown to ten feet tall when they were walking on all four feet. They didn't care too much about the run; all they really cared about was making their grandpa happy. Before the race, Jebadiya constructed two massive hamster balls in the back of the cave and asked his grandsons to get inside.

In town, Jebadiya's son Ronald was in one of the cages closest to Rumpus's seat high up in the tree. It was time for revenge, and it was time to give a new meaning to the term Running of the Hamsters.

Back in the cave, Jebadiya and his grandsons could faintly hear the mayor and the crowd. The seals were locked, and the boys were ready to go. The sound of an airhorn blasted down the road.

"It's finally here!" the tiny hamster screamed as he tried to push the thin log holding the two twenty-foot-tall hamster balls in place. He pushed with all his might until the log finally gave way with a pop of Jebadiya's lower back.

The two boys scuttled down the ramp inside the balls, picking up speed, soon flying toward the tiny cave hole. Down in the town, the race had begun, and a wave of red sashes were jogging and turning around, pointing at the hamsters as they made their way down the cobblestone street. Rumpus watched in awe and couldn't help but laugh at the whole spectacle of it all—until he heard the loud crash up the mountain. With all the people in the town yelling and the music playing so loud, no one heard the noise from the mountainside. Squinting, he could see two huge plastic balls bouncing down the hillside, making their way into the road and bounding to the town's circle.

Ronald the hamster could feel the rumble in the ground growing. With a smile, he stopped, put his two fingers under his teeth, and whistled. All the hamsters stopped at once, and all looked back at the same time. They then split on both sides, running into the crowds and leaving the runners slowing in confusion.

As Rumpus and Sunny realized what they were seeing, Sunny flew up, hovering next to Rumpus, who stood on his branch, holding onto the base of the tree to keep his balance as the ground shook. "Do you see what I see?" Sunny screamed over at Rumpus.

"Is this what always happens?" Rumpus yelled back over the noise.

"Nope! This is something brand new—but isn't it fantastic?" Sunny yelled back in delight.

The two massive hamster balls collided into the first people, who screamed as they tried to get out of the way. Creatures left and right were pummeled as the two balls bounced off of buildings, bringing some of them to the ground and causing total chaos in the streets.

Vendor carts were crushed, and balloons everywhere started to rise into the atmosphere. Their music drowned out by screams, the band scattered all over the town's center while the two balls made their way down the next level of the road.

Sunny looked up to Rumpus and hollered, "Jump on my back and let's follow the show!"

Rumpus jumped onto her back, and Agape followed them in the direction of the two wrecking balls bouncing through the town like a pinball machine.

Jebadiya sat farther up the mountain watching the show with his drink and telescope, almost unable to breathe through his laughter. This was the best day of his life, and two years of dedication were finally paying off. "Run, Hamster Run!" he screamed out in glee and took a long sip from his cocktail.

Back in the town, Rumpus and his friends chased the insanity rolling down the road, and some red-sashed runners dropped like flies while others ran harder than they ever had before. Jason's hamster ball hit a large building about three quarters of the way down and got wedged into a tall tower at the front of the library. He quickly turned around in his bubble and started pushing on the other side, rocking back and forth until he popped free and resumed his rolling downhill journey. After a series of pops and cracks, the building started to topple, as if a giant lumberjack had chopped out the lower section.

Rumpus yelled from Sunny's back to the people below, "Run, run...it's coming down!" With a mighty smash, the library crashed down, sending a shockwave of a pink dust cloud in every direction. Books and boards scattered into the street. None of them, unfortunately for Rumpus, were the field guide; he'd half expected it to magically reveal itself in that moment.

They continued to follow the hamster balls down the hill, Rumpus gasping and Sunny laughing her beak off. It wasn't particularly nice to laugh at what was going on, but flying through the air, Sunny couldn't help but find the surprised looks on so many faces hilarious. They balls were starting to run out of road and runners to squish when the two hamsters came back side by side and noticed one more runner hauling butt down the road, gulping air like he was drowning. The two brothers, looking at each other with devilish grins, picked up the pace and charged at the last runner on the road.

This last runner was a land octopus named Orville, cousin to the famous trainer on the island named Coach Manos. Orville was kind of a tattletale, and if there was anyone who deserved to be squished, it was him. He zigged and zagged, with the two brothers taking turns getting inches away from him.

At the last bend in the road at the end of the town was a huge statue of Mynusha's most famous inhabitant, Stubbornous the Great. He was the boxing champ of the island. The statue featured the champ holding up a giant cupcake with his boxing gloves on. One glove said LOVE and the other said HATE. The statue stood eighteen feet tall, including the stone base. Orville was running straight for it, looking back at the two hamster balls barreling down on him. He cleared a speed bump, but the two death balls hit it like a ramp, sending them flying into the air. Orville saw what was happening and had the clarity of mind to come screeching to a halt and watch the two spinning brothers fly over his head, blocking out the suns. Don tried to look back, and his face was squished up against the plastic cage, watching Orville in slow motion. The two plastic spheres landed on each side of the sculpture, cracking it loose from the foundation. With the weight of the cupcake over his head, the champ fell forward as the two plastic crushing machines continued down the side of the mountain into the valley below. Orville was now looking uphill, right toward Rumps and the crew, when the statue landed square on his head, leaving nothing but jelly and legs shooting in all directions.

The griffin turned his body toward the hole, sticking his head down and giving it the side eye. "Well, looky looky here, my friend. We might have never found it if it weren't for these wacky hamsters today.

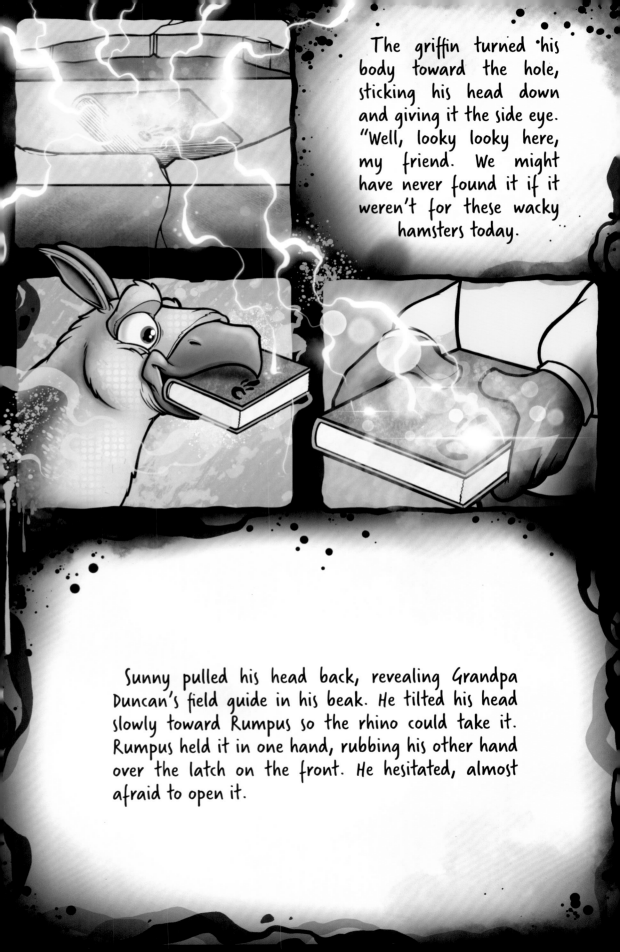

Sunny pulled his head back, revealing Grandpa Duncan's field guide in his beak. He tilted his head slowly toward Rumpus so the rhino could take it. Rumpus held it in one hand, rubbing his other hand over the latch on the front. He hesitated, almost afraid to open it.

"If we don't get out of here soon, they're going to think *we* broke this statue," Sunny piped up. She latched her claws around Rumpus's shoulders again and flew back up the road, Agape followed them as they glided over the destruction. Rumpus couldn't take his eyes off the book, despite flying over many passed-out runners, broken carts, smashed cupcakes, and demolished buildings. He didn't even notice the one guy who never missed any party on the island. Walrusamus the Party Walrus looked up from a pile of rubble and took notice of the rhino he'd met in the fields.

The trio passed over the town, flying over old Jebadiya sitting in this lounge chair. The hamster mastermind jumped up as they passed over him, and Rumpus broke eye contact with his new prize

to see a hysterical old hamster dancing with a drink and cane howling, "RUN, Hamster RUN! Ahhh hahahahahahaha!"

Sunny banked left, and they were off to the forest below. They'd had a full day, and the suns were getting low. "Rumpus, we need to get you down to a safe place tonight," Sunny said. "I got the perfect spot in the forest at the base of the mountains where we can crash before I send you on your way. Get that book into your backpack before you drop it."

There was no way Rumpus was ever going to drop it. He ignored Sunny and squeezed the book tightly to his chest as if he were hugging his grandpa again. The griffin let him have his moment with the book as the three of them glided down the rocks along the cliffside of the Arion Ater Mountains.

CHAPTER 11

IT'S MY PARTY AND I'LL CRY IF I WANT TO

Walrusamus the Party Walrus was a little freaked out. Rumpus was obviously way off the beaten path the walrus had sent him on, and General Vonhareliar was going to be really pissed to find out Walrusamus hadn't fully followed through on watching him leave, or even guided him there himself. Now he was at an impasse. Should he go looking for Rumpus? Or should he call in the sighting himself? On the one hand, by calling it in he would be ripping the band-aid right off *and* be doing his job. On the other hand, if he went looking for Rumpus and found him, then he might be able to fix the situation, and no one would ever know. Of course, there was a chance that the general already knew, given all the spies and cameras on the island, so that could be a serious risk as well. Walrusamus started to panic in indecision when his one good eye caught one of the knocked-over carts with a cage of cupcakes and ale. Walrusamus looked back and forth to see if anyone was around. He could hear some of the village folks moaning in the distance, so he took a chance and waddled over to the cart. "Just borrowing this to help with my stress," he justified to himself. The walrus gently reached into the cage to pick a cupcake and poured a large ale into his mouth.

There was no way to know if it really helped the situation, but it sure helped him not mind so much for a second. As he sat down to think about his next move, a bunch of villagers walked up and joined him. Within minutes, a full-blown party broke out around him. He was starting to have fun when someone in the crowd said in a drunken slur, "Most…epic…hamster…run…ever," and then started crying.

The whole crowd went from happy to sad in moments, which freaked out the walrus, who had almost forgotten his responsibilities. Realizing he was in no condition to hunt down Rumpus, he blubbered out, "Does anyone have a way I can make a call into the capital?"

Walrusamus sat down in the middle of all the sad villagers and joined the crowd of crying party poopers.

Up the next ridge of mountains, Sunny, Rumpus and Agape were working their way to the top to follow the winding tip. "Where are we going, Sunny?" Rumpus gasped, trying to catch his breath in the cold air.

"We are going to the town of Soulsummit, Rumpus. Your grandpa had several hiding spots that a couple of us knew about, and I thought that you might want to spend the night in a place your grandpa would sometimes sleep in. It's a very secluded town mostly full of monks. It's almost impossible to get up to, and for the most part full of people who will either pay us no mind at all or are friends in the way that they don't want anything to do with the direction the island has gone in over the years. It's safe, Rumpus, and a perfect place to gather your thoughts."

Rumpus looked off to the side as Sunny glided back and forth. The rocks were shades of glittered purple, deep blue purples, and stripes of plum. He was captured by the beauty of it all and made eye contact with Agape. "That sounds really nice. What do you think, buddy?"

Agape nodded with a smile and turned back to her gliding, elevating up over them.

The group traveled in silence for awhile, enjoying the quiet. A lot had happened to the three of them over the last thirty-six hours. It was nice to not be worrying about creatures, a fire, or giant hamsters rolling over a village. The sound of the cool air was melodically broken by a series of hums near the cliff they flew toward. Rumpus noticed a group of creatures in the distance and listened harder, trying to place the music. The closest thing he could compare it to was a mix of Tibetan throat singing and beatboxing. Rumpus was entranced as they came into closer view.

"We must be getting close!" yelled out Sunny to her passenger. "Those are the mountain species of a special animal on the island called the longsong bittengullets. It's been said that they have been on the island longer than any of the different kinds of creatures here." As the group passed the cliffside, Rumpus took in the sight of these majestic singers. Their tones of blue complimented the mountain's purples. Their blob-like bodies looked like squeezed out soft serve ice cream, with toothy toad faces stuck on the front. One singer's body had stripes of white winter fur standing on four long, thin, fleshy deer-like legs. The creatures looked to Rumpus to be three to four feet tall. Sunny started to turn away

from the cliffside and fly out into the open air. For the first time since seeing the bittengullets, Rumpus looked down and realized how high they actually were. Through the mist and clouds Rumpus could barely even see the ground.

"Hold on, my man" yelled out Sunny. "We are coming back around to the cliffs!" She pulled a hard bank left, back to the singers, who were now silent. "This is where you come in, Rumpus! If I am right, then I'm pretty sure this should work..." Sunny pulled up and hovered in front of the group of about thirty singers, all perched on different levels of the sheer cliff. "Your grandpa had an arrangement with these guys, but it's been some years, so I hope this works. If it doesn't, we'll have to go through town, and even though I know that they should all be friends, like I said...it's been some years."

The captive audience leaned in toward Sunny and the confused Rumpus. "What am I supposed to do?" Rumpus asked.

Sunny cocked her head back like birds do and looked up at him with one eye. "We need you to sing, my friend."

"I don't sing, Sunny," chuckled the tired rhino.

Sunny ignored him. "Your grandpa was one of the greatest to ever visit the island, but I wouldn't have called him a singer either," she said with a laugh. "He did have a song that he shared a little too much, and if you were like us, then you may have heard it more times than you would have liked. It was sweet, but he was a terrible singer. I'm hoping you are just as bad, and they think that you are him."

Rumpus instantly knew what song Sunny was talking about. When they would get in his old truck and go on their field trips, his grandpa would often sing it over and over, almost as if he knew it was driving the young Rumpus a little crazy. His voice would lower and turn to gravel and crack. It was almost like he was doing a parody of an old cowboy around the campfire. The problem was his grandpa would sing just the first part of the song over and over again. He never sang anymore after the first chorus. Later Rumpus learned that his grandpa loved the tune and how it made him think of another time, but he hated a line that referred disparagingly to the indigenous people of the Americas. He hated slurs and hated the bullies who came up with them.

"Home on the Range," Rumpus whispered quietly, with a slight melody.

"We need you to channel your grandpa and do it just as obnoxiously as he did," Sunny pushed. "It's the only way they have ever heard it, and I hope the version you know matches! Start from the beginning!"

Rumpus looked around and summoned a little courage. "Ohhhh, give me a home…" he sheepishly sang as he made eye contact with one of the bittengullets. When all four of the creatures' eyes squinted and concentrated on Rumpus, it made him stop. Their eyes all started to glow a little bit.

"We need to try and sound like your grandpa in every way possible, Rumpus!" Sunny yelled out in exasperation.

Rumpus closed his eyes and pictured his grandpa driving his truck down Highway 69, singing without a care in the world. He pulled in his breath, and just as he was about to sing, Agape flew over and gave him a little bite on the back of the leg.

"OHHHHH!" Rumpus belted out, way louder than he'd been about to sing. Looking down with a smile, he continued "GIIIVE MEEEE AAAAA HOOOOOMMMME!" It was an almost perfect impression of Grandpa Duncan.

"Shhhhhh," whispered Sunny before he could continue. Rumpus had finally loosened up enough to have fun with it and was taken back by the request to stop. All the longsong bittengullets now looked straight at them with glowing eyes. Some of them stood, and others turned to face them; in unison, they started to jitter and shake. Then, all at once, they sang what sort of sounded like the next line, but low and monotone with all of the words joined together; it was almost more of a hummed melody. Rumpus knew it was the line "where the buffalo roam"—but again, it sounded like Tibetan throat beatboxing. Then there was total silence.

The adventurers and the bittengullets all stared at each other for what seemed like an eternity until Rumpus broke the silence. "Is that it?"

A grumble shook the cliffside, and all the bittengullets looked up, causing the team to

follow their eyes. A rock rolled sideways to reveal a cave in the side of the cliff, and like that, Sunny's wings caught a current, lifting them to the entrance, where they landed in the mouth of the cave.

Agape flew in like she owned the place. There was an old, giant switch with a wooden handle sticking

out from the cave wall, and Agape landed on it, jerking her body downward to lower the switch until it touched the stone. Light after light down the tunnel turned on until Rumpus could see a large, wooden door down at the end.

"So, I'm going to have to take off for a little bit and check in with my boss," Sunny announced. "I can promise you this right now: it's going to be ok. You'll be safe here—it's one of your grandpa's safest hiding spots on the island. Agape will stay with you tonight, and I will be back first thing in the morning." Sunny put a wing on Rumpus's shoulder. "This is a great chance for you to look at that book and all his other stuff. I think you'll be excited to see it! So just hang tight. A ladder in there goes up into the town, but wait until you hear from me. Tomorrow morning, we will get you on the right path, my friend."

Rumpus looked over at Sunny and smiled. "Sounds good to me. Thank you so much for your help."

As Sunny turned around and flew off, the stone started to roll back. Rumpus turned his attention to some writing on the wall above the switch. "Where the deer and the antelope play" was scribbled there like bathroom graffiti. Rumpus placed his hand on the words and smiled, turning his head to the door as Agape landed on his shoulder. Together, they walked down the mine tunnel.

When they got to the end, they were in a small, round room with a door. To the left of the door was a small shelf with a record player, and below it a crate of records. Rumpus reached out to the door and yanked on the handle, but it was locked. The light above the record player flickered, and Rumpus noticed more words on the wall right above the records: "Where seldom is heard, a discouraging word."

Agape flew over to the records and started picking through the stack, flipping them in the old milk crate. Rumpus crouched next to her. "What record is it?"

The bird just shrugged her shoulders and fluffed up, pecking her beak on the stack.

"OK, Grandpa Duncan… what am I looking for here?" Rumpus flipped through the records, and at first nothing stuck out—until he stopped on an old 45 titled "This Little Light of Mine," sung by Sister Rosetta Tharpe. Rumpus grinned from ear to ear. "I see what you did, Grandpa." If there was a second song that his grandpa loved the most, this was it. He never sang the words, but it was something he would hum all the time. Rumpus carefully blew the dust off the record and placed it on the turntable.

He picked up the needle and set it on the record.

Rumpus had never heard this version of the song. It opened with an upbeat swing, and Tharpe started playing an electric guitar. Her lyrics filled the room as twelve speakers around him near the ceiling sang out, "This little light of mine, I'm going to let it shine!" Glowing letters on the door appeared, saying, "And the skies are not cloudy all day." As the "Y" in day illuminated, a series of locks and mechanisms sprang into action. The door opened, revealing one of the hideouts of the famous adventurer.

CHAPTER 12

MICROPHONE CHECK, MICRO-MICROPHONE CHECKA

On another part of the island, General Von Hareliar paced the halls of the Telegenic Dome, waiting for an update when the radio finally chirped in down the hall.

"Party Walrus to TD1. Party Walrus to TD1. Do you copy?"

General Von Hareliar was usually a rabbit of composure, but considering the circumstances and the boss he had to report to, he sprinted down to the hall. Just as the radio operator was about to answer, the general's hand gripped his dopey face and threw him across the room into the wall. Slamming into the chair, his finger on the button of the microphone, General Von Hareliar answered, "Go on. TD1."

Party Walrus paused nervously on the other side. That voice sounded very familiar. As he tried to remember where he had heard this voice, his inner thoughts were interrupted by reality. "This is General Von Hareliar," the voice continued. "Camera is now on, Mr. Walrus, and I suggest you get to it."

Party Walrus gulped slowly, and his shaking flipper tapped out an SOS in Morse code on the microphone button before he finally pushed it all the way down. "Good...good evening, sir. Party Walrus reporting..."

"And?" the general snapped back.

The trembling walrus leaned in and sheepishly answered. "I'm in Mynusha to keep an eye on the annual Hamster Run, and the rhino was spotted here."

"And is there a reason why you are not *with* the rhino, escorting him to Limerick Cove?" popped back through the speaker. The general's low, calm voice scared Party Walrus even more. He froze up again and just stared at the microphone. "WELL?" The word screamed back through the speaker, sending the mic flipping back and forth between Walrusamus's hands.

"I...I thought you might want me to tell him where to go...and also keep an eye on one of the biggest parties or the year?"

"YOU. HAD. ONE. JOB! And what kind of idiot thinks—"

Party Walrus scrambled to hide behind a chair, his eyes glued to the speaker, but the line went dead. He slowly emerged from behind the chair and started tapping the microphone button.

On the other side of the line was a general losing his mind. He forgot about the length of cord on the microphone and started walking with it. When the line snapped in the middle of his rant to the incompetent walrus, he found himself holding the broken mic. This sent him over the edge, causing him to launch the mic straight into the face of the rabbit radio operator, who had finally come to from his last encounter with the general. Not yet satisfied with his destruction, the general picked up the chair, slamming it into pieces on the floor. Then he noticed the camera feed and Walrusamus coming out from behind his chair on the other side. He started screaming at the screen as if the terrified walrus could hear him. "When I see you…I'm… I'm going to take that stupid party hat and shove it some place you don't like it and then crush you into a million pieces!"

Even though Party Walrus couldn't hear the general on the other end, he happened to look up at the camera and knew that nothing good was happening or going to happen. He shuddered at the thought of what was being said but forced a grin and saluted into the camera as if he'd gotten orders and was still in good graces.

Both sides of the conversation did almost the exact same thing at the same time. Walrusamus radioed into another tower near Mynusha, giving instruction for bees to be released from several stations to fly toward Limerick Cove, looking for Rumpus. The general screamed down the hall to the other guards, "Someone fix this radio and call the stations around Limerick Cove! Have bees search for this rhino and spread out toward Mynusha."

The Party Walrus walked in circles. He knew that he should have just gone with Rumpus when he had the chance, but the combination of being lazy and the excitement of being the one to break the news about the visitor had made him lose sight of what he should have done to make it go right. Combined with all the different ales and cupcakes over the last couple days—and his favorite party of the year with the hamsters—it was enough to make him forget any priority. Still, he did have one job to do, and it was a pretty relaxed assignment compared to the pressure he had faced before he was fired for his mental breakdown in his last job. (But that's another story altogether.)

*U*p in the mountains and out of sight below the town of Soulsummit, Rumpus explored his grandpa's hideout. There was a large, comfy bed covered in multicolored furs and a large, handmade wooden desk covered in drawings and pictures. Several were pinned to the wall, including a picture of Rumpus as a kid. Rumpus was in awe of this whole life that his grandpa had found and how closely it resembled the one he always joked he should have lived.

Emotions washed over Rumpus. Now he knew why he'd never seen his grandpa again. He couldn't help but wonder if that also meant *he* would never make it back to Kansas City again.

He remembered how, for a time, he was so angry at his grandpa. He'd thought that his grandpa had abandoned all of them. Other times, he thought something bad had happened to him, since the police had never found a trace after his disappearance. Rumpus stopped himself from getting too upset and walked over to empty cupboards, opening the door to an empty deco-looking icebox fridge. A glance back to the bed reminded him of the field guide that had been such a big deal to find. "Let's see what Grandpa was up to the last several years and if there are any clues in there."

Rumpus sat back on the bed and turned on the lamp, noticing a small radio and microphone next to it. Agape flew over and started making a nest in the furs at the bottom of the bed, wasting no time going to sleep. The rhino's thick fingers flipped through the pages in the sketchbook filled with drawings and descriptions. Some pages just had creatures with notes about things to stay away from or things that were good about them. There were plants with

a lot of the same kind of information next to them. More pages looked like full journal entries of what Grandpa Duncan did that day. Rumpus stopped on one that looked interesting.

> Today was a hard day. The cupcakes on the island are basically all gone, and no one knows where. The level of addiction and anger brings out the worst in the inhabitants all over the island. All over, rumors are causing friendships to break apart in desperation. I'm so glad I don't have a sweet tooth, and that Leonidas warned me about the pitfalls of eating cupcakes!
>
> There are stories of a singular cupcake being kept out in the middle of the small desert near the Bitter Dunes. The worst of the worst are traveling to that part of the island to try to find it. This will only lead to an incredible and epic feud—no good is going to come from that many violent creatures. I'm going to have to investigate further.

FUZZAKELS —

- PINK VERSIONS FOUND NEAR BERGSLAG SUGAR.

- WHITE VERSIONS FOUND NEAR LIMERICK COVE.

12-18 INCHES TALL

18 INCHES WIDE

CARNIVORUS SUN PITCHER — LOW TO THE GROUND... BIT MY LEG THE OTHER DAY. KNOWN TO EAT BEES ...

– LIONAPEDE –

3 INCHES

– TODAY WAS A HARD DAY. THE CUPCAKES ON THE
ISLAND ARE BASICALLY ALL GONE, AND NO ONE
KNOWS WHERE. THE LEVEL OF ADDICTION AND
ANGER BRINGS OUT THE WORST IN THE WHABITANTS
ALL OVER THE ISLAND. ALL OVER, RUMORS ARE
CAUSING FRIENDSHIPS TO BREAK APART IN DESPERATION.
I'M SO GLAD I DON'T HAVE A SWEET TOOTH, AND THAT
LEONITAS WARNED ME ABOUT THE PITFALLS OF EATING
CUPCAKES!

THERE ARE STORIES OF A SINGULAR CUPCAKE BEING
KEPT OUT IN THE MIDDLE OF THE SMALL DESERT
NEAR THE BITTER DUNES. THE WORST OF THE WORST
ARE TRAVELING TO THAT PART OF THE ISLAND TO TRY
TO FIND IT. THIS WILL ONLY LEAD TO AN INCREDIBLE
AND EPIC FEUD. – NO GOOD IS GOING TO COME
FROM THAT MANY VIOLENT CREATURES...
I'M GOING TO HAVE TO INVESTIGATE FURTHER.

GLOW SHROOMS –
ARION ATER
MOUNTAINS –

4 INCHES

Rumpus couldn't help but skip around in the journal out of curiosity. One entry talked about bringing sketches to reality and the power of other dimensional fingers. A whole page was dedicated to different levels of cupcakes Grandpa had seen and how they slowly evolved to sprout arms in legs over time if no one ate them. There was so much to read—but the bed was so comfy. Rumpus never could read in bed without falling asleep. It didn't take long before he drifted off, sleeping soundly with his face tucked into fur blankets that smelled like his grandpa.

Hours passed before he was woken by the radio on the stand. "Rumpus. Rumpus, do you copy?" He rubbed his eyes and sat up, looking blankly at the radio and the microphone. "If you can hear me, Rumpus, you just push the button on the mic to talk back."

Rumpus swung his legs around off the side of the bed, curious about who was calling him. "Umm go on, Rumpus?" he answered with a rise in his voice, like he wasn't sure who he was.

"Hey, my friend! It's your favorite lion buddy. It's dinner time, and you gotta be getting hungry, so come on up and let's grab some ramen!"

Rumpus looked around the room for a place that would allow him to go up. He started walking back to the front door when Agape flew in front of him, stopping him in his tracks. The bee eater flew over to a perch and landed with some force, triggering a circular trap door in the ceiling to open. Rumpus walked over to the door in the ceiling and looked up into a tunnel with a ladder leading up to the surface. The hatch opened at the top to reveal the happy face of his friend Leonidas peeking over the edge. "You hungry, mister?"

Rumpus laughed. "You know it, man. Always down for some ramen!" Rumpus grabbed his backpack and threw in the field guide and some sketches off the desk, then jumped up onto the ladder to go streetside. Agape flew up before him, and the big, hungry rhino climbed the ladder.

CHAPTER 13

RAMEN FOR THE SOUL

Rumpus emerged in the back of the small kitchen of a ramen shop. "I knew I smelled something wonderful when I was coming up," he said. Leonidas closed the hatch behind him, and Rumpus noticed that in the evening light, he couldn't even see where the door was anymore—but who cared, with those savory smells all around him?

"Welcome to Madam Shownuff's Ramen Spot!" Leonidas said with excitement.

"Wait a minute," said Rumpus with confusion. "Madam Shownuff? Didn't we go to another one called Madam FoSho in the Olive Jar Jungle?"

The jolly lion laughed and looked back as he waved Rumpus around the bar side to the pull-up seats. "Yeah, man, there are a bunch of them around the island and they are all cousins, or sisters, or something like that. The most important thing to remember is that you will always have the best all

natural meals if the name of the ramen spot starts with Madam. Haha! Shownuff!"

Leonidas pulled out a chair. "Grab a seat, my friend, and let me handle the order."

Rumpus smiled and took a seat. "It's good to see you, Leo. Appreciate the dinner."

The wise lion placed an order by yelling out to the kitchen, then stopped and smiled at the rested rhino sitting next to him. "It's good to see you a little more refreshed and settled in, Rumpus. I know this has been a lot for you to take in, and I hope sending some time in one of your grandpa's spots gave you some comfort."

Rumpus smiled and adjusted himself into the seat, leaning hard on the bar and noticing Agape perched on the sign above him. "I'm feeling a lot better, Leo. I wish we knew where my grandpa was, but as often as I said I wanted an escape from my boring life, I can see why he was able to make a life here. The field guide I have is proof of something we used to talk about when I was a kid."

The lion looked down at his arms and hands resting on the bar. "El Vaquero, your grandpa, was just a straight up amazing man, and many of us miss him dearly. I see him all over you, and that both excites me and makes me worried. I'm sure it makes some other people worried too. We need to talk about what you should expect on this island."

Two bowls of fresh ramen showed up in front of them, and Rumpus grabbed on to the deep spoon. "You have any idea what happened to my grandpa?"

The lion sighed while stirring his ramen. "I wish I had a real answer for you, brother, but I just don't. Maybe we can figure that out together. Nothing would make me happier than to find out that he is still alive and well and reunite the two of you."

Rumpus slurped up some broth and felt the warmth work its way down. "It seems like he made an impression. When I get the chance to sit longer and go through his field guide, I'm hoping to learn so much more about him. What did he do here that made him a target, I guess, and what do I have to worry about?"

"Well, Rumpus, I know you got the chance to meet Sunny and spend time down the beach. Your grandpa was the first person in years to repair what he called a phone in that giant area surrounded by the thorns that the army planted. That was the first time in years that anyone got to start talking to the Maker again."

Leonidas leaned back, reminiscing. "It was literally the launch of a revolution," he continued. "The field you were dropped off in, called the Resound Fields, actually had a DJ show up again and start playing music. That caused a lot of panic, and a bunch of people we loved lost their lives when General Von Hareliar and his goon patrol showed up. This was all happening while the cupcakes were disappearing. Your grandpa's need to help people was not part of the master plan for the powers that be. The last time we saw your grandpa, he was heading for the Bitter Dunes to see why so many of our island's biggest criminals were after a single cupcake."

Rumpus and Leonidas sat in silence and ate their ramen. That was a lot to take in, and Rumpus had a feeling there was so much more to all of it.

"Baby," a voice interrupted their love affair with their food. "No one is saying it right out, but the word is spreading. There are people on this island hoping you pick up where your grandpa left off." A large, stout creature with four arms, no neck, and a flowered apron appeared on the other side of the bar. "You are the spitting image of him, you know.

Me and him had a special relationship, if you know what I mean?"

Rumpus glanced over at Leo, whose eyes had grown large, shaking his head and biting his lip behind his paw as if no one could see. "Shut up, Leonidas, or you can make your own dinner from now on," she barked sideways while still sending a love-filled gaze toward Rumpus.

The shy rhino blushed. "Ma'am, this is the best ramen I have ever had."

The cook paused, then started laughing. "Boy, are you proposing to me or what? I think I can read between those lines," she belted out. As she turned around, her giant butt knocked stuff over in every direction, and the shop's other employee desperately tried to keep up with her caboose.

Rumpus looked at Leonidas, and the pair shared a silent laugh. "Your grandpa had all the ladies chasing after him," Leonidas whispered.

"I don't chase after no one, ya old lion goat!" Madam Shownuff yelled out from the back of the kitchen.

"What the heck am I supposed to do next?" asked Rumpus.

"That's something your grandfather used to ask all the time," Leonidas answered with a grin. "But I think what he came to is what you need to find for yourself. You just need to live your life, Rumpus. That field guide in your backpack is proof of your grandpa doing that very thing. Even though he was in a new place that was hostile at times and there was no known way home, he did things he loved. The reason he was so famous was that he did just that, and when it came time to do the right thing, you could always count on him. He didn't go looking for a fight, but he finished more than we could count. If he felt called to action, he obeyed that calling, and if he wanted to go on a solo adventure and do his exploring and drawing, then he did it with wisdom. Maybe you should ask yourself what *you* want to do, and see where life takes you."

Rumpus loved hearing these things about his grandpa. He'd grown up wanting the same things but wasn't good at verbalizing them. He was stuck in a boring job and would draw on his breaks. He also wanted some adventure.

"Is there anything that you want to do, Rumpus?"

Rumpus drank down the rest of his broth and looked over with the bowl still at his lips. Setting his dry bowl down, he answered. "I read some stuff in his field guide about bringing sketches to life, and something called Dimensional Fingers."

"That's a pretty big start, Rumpus. It requires the pen. Is that in the loop of the field guide?"

He didn't remember a pen, so he pulled the field guide out of his backpack. "Here it is, but I don't see a pen."

Leonidas let out a little laugh. "You are so much like him. Go big or go home, he would say sometimes. The pen your grandpa used was from a shop down in Limerick Cove. It takes a special squid ink from the cove that some of the pirates bring in, and your grandpa seemed to think that played a big part in the process. Personally, I think it requires more faith than ink, but having that ink seemed to make him feel better about it. If we go down to the Cove, we have to be really careful, Rumpus. It's one of the most dangerous places on the island, crawling with pirates, island security, bees who work for different Bakers, and collectors—those who specialize in collecting the varied cupcakes that have evolved on the island. You could disappear or get lost forever in the cove. We have to stay on our toes!"

"If my grandpa thought it was important, then so do I," Rumpus said. "I'm not really sure what I'm doing, but I feel like it's important that I build on what he did."

The lion placed his hand on the rhino's. "Well, son, we are going to have to find you a disguise. Looking the way we do will draw a lot of attention; I'm supposed to be chained to a rock, if you remember. This is going to be a fun trip, but we have to be really careful.

The friends stepped back from their seats, and while Leonidas paid for dinner and made jokes, Rumpus looked around. The old stone streets were filled with all kinds of unique Nisamaheans eating and shopping at little merchants in the middle of the tiny town. He noticed that some of them were staring at him with smiles. He guessed they all thought he looked like their hero, El Vaquero.

The town up on the top of the mountain only had a couple hundred residents. They were secluded because it was such a pain to get up there. That made it one of the few places on the island that was not really watched, and for the most part they were free and self-sufficient.

"We are all squared away, my friend," Leonidas said. "Let's tuck past the bar back into the kitchen and get back down to your grandpa's place. I know he had several disguises. Then we can figure out how we are going to get down to the cove. It's a long way down there."

The two of them went back down to the secret lair, and Leonidas grabbed some cloaks with hoods and threw them on the chair. "Get some sleep, Rumpus," the old lion advised. "Tomorrow, you can wear your grandpa's old cloak and hood. I'm going to head up and grab a room myself. I'll be back in the morning." As the lion started back up the ladder, Rumpus lay on the bed. His head rested on part of the cloak, and he could swear that he smelled the spearmint gum his grandpa always chewed, mixed with the scent of pipe tobacco. He opened the field guide and started to read. Even though he wanted to read it all that night, he quickly drifted off to sleep.

CHAPTER 14

DOWN TO THE INKWELL WITH A SONG

The next morning Rumpus woke early and walked down to the opening in the cave. He sat on the ledge and looked down onto the thin clouds rolling by under his feet. Opening the field guide, he read some more. His eyes made their way to an entry above a drawing of what looked like a floating motorcycle.

Today I brought a drawing out of the field guide with the help—I think—of this new pen with the squid ink from the cove. Leonidas says it's something more, but what else could it be besides this ink? He told me that this ability has not been seen on the island in a couple of generations—it's considered a children's tale told to spark the imagination. But that old lion figured I might be able to do it. He told me to grab the sketch with the edges of my fingers, concentrate and have faith, and pull it out. To humor him, I drew a plunger. To my surprise, it worked. That's how I now have One Ton the plunger.

Rumpus smiled and looked over at the plunger sticking out of his backpack. Agape was sitting on his back, watching him read a book he was probably more familiar with than anyone. It was too bad the bee eater couldn't say more than her name.

Rumpus started to turn another page when his concentration was broken by a familiar voice. "Good morning, my friend! Are you ready to go get into some trouble?" The lion threw the cloak disguise at him. "Toss that into your backpack. We're going for a ride on something your grandpa designed." While Rumpus packed away his cloak, Leonidas went to the side of the cave entrance and pulled off a couple backpacks. "Rumpus, you are going to have to wear your other pack on the front so we can wear these on our backs."

"What am I looking at here, Leo?" Rumpus asked as he figured out how to wear both packs.

"It's just one of the many wonderful things your grandfather drew and brought into being. We have done this jump a bunch of times."

The rhino's face changed from interested to concerned as he looked out of the mouth of the cave. All he could see were clouds. "Did…did you just say jump?"

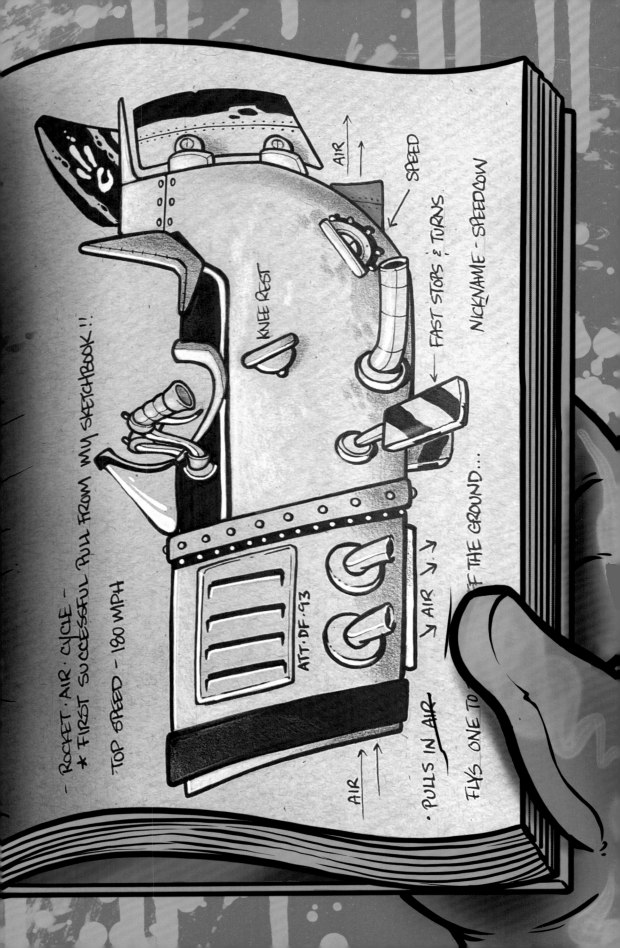

The trippy lion brushed his mane to the side, revealing his eyeball for the first time, his pupil looking down. With a belly laugh of excitement, he answered with a yes as he leaned back and did a trust fall out of the cave, tumbling into a cloud below with a POOF!

"LEO!!" Rumpus screamed in surprise. Before he could finish saying his name, the lion sprang back up through the clouds once again, laughing and flying right in front of the cave's mouth. The backpack now had a pair of wings flapping on each side, helping him hover in place.

"Just think about it, Rumpus! You could be drawing things like this and bringing them into being—but it's going to require a leap of faith, my young friend!"

After that fright of an experience, the young rhino had grabbed tightly to the edge of the tunnel, like he had just now realized how high up he actually was.

"You take that leap, and the backpack will take over the rest for you," Leonidas promised. "It's going to take some faith and trust in what your grandpa made. We really need to get going down to the market at Limerick Cove when it opens. The

later it gets, there will be more soldiers and pirates, and it will be harder to stay unnoticed."

Agape flew over and landed on Rumpus's shoulder, giving him a rub on the cheek before she took flight out of the cave and spun around, waving Rumpus out with his colorful wing. Rumpus took a step up to the ledge. All he could see was clouds, which was helpful, but it also sent his imagination into overdrive about how high he might be. Thinking about how wild this ride had been, after all the things he had seen so far, the discovery that his grandpa had been here before proved that more was possible than Rumpus had ever imagined. "Well, here goes nothing," Rumpus sighed as he was about to step off the edge.

"No, stop!" yelled Leo. "Here goes something! What you are doing is *not* nothing!"

Rumpus stopped and nodded. Leonidas was right: this had all really been something. Consciously aware of his eyes almost closing as he stepped out, he thought in that split second about how real faith might require seeing where he was going. With eyes wide open he stepped off the ledge toward the lion and the bird cheering him on. He felt the winds pick up on his cheeks as he started to free fall into

the cloud right below. Before he had a chance to think about the fact that he was going down and not up, the wings unfurled from the sides of the backpack, sending a jerk through his body and his legs swinging out. The rhino grabbed onto the shoulder straps like he was in a parachute and gasped for air. Agape flew by, winking at him and chattering melodically.

Leonidas flew up next to him. "Great job, my young and heavy friend! You look like you know what you are doing, haha!"

Rumpus looked down at his legs just as a couple clouds parted. He must have been miles up in the air. He quickly set his eyes forward as two hard wires with handles and buttons sprang from the sides of the packs. "The pack will take you in the direction you want it to go," Leonidas explained. "It can sense what you want to do. The right-hand button will speed you up; the left will slow you down. Both at the same time will bring the wings in for a dive." And just like that Leonidas looked up and leaned back into a backflip, barrel rolling several times and diving between the clouds below as Agape followed close behind. "Come on, Rumpus!" his voice echoed. "It's time to get moving!"

Rumpus looked around at how he was hovering and cracked a huge smile. He puffed up his chest, gripped the controls, and hit both buttons at once as he pointed his head down. Off he shot like a rocket. Breaking the underbelly of the cotton-like blanket of clouds, he could see the side of the mountain. Pumping the break switch, he slowed into a glide down the mountainside as the wings on his backpack popped out once more. The purples in the rocks faded away into a reddish-brown landscape with small, skinny trees. The trees grew denser until they flew over a whole jungle.

"This way, Rumpus!" the lion yelled, banking right to run parallel with the ocean in the distance.

They traveled the coastline. Rumpus marveled at the view, watching ships come into port. Leonidas swerved to fly closer to the rhino, the two of them parallel over the ground.

"We are getting close, Rumpus!" Leonidas called. "We need to stay a little bit low to come around the backside of the port. We'll land a ways out and walk from there. Your grandpa has a spot where he used to hide some things right outside of the port."

As they flew closer, small openings in the trees showed Rumpus some of the creatures traveling in and out to one of the island's busiest trading posts. He noticed that Leonidas was descending toward the trees, so he followed as Agape spiraled around the two of them in perfect circles.

The dynamic trio landed behind a small rock formation not too far from the port. Agape touched down on a short, squatty tree and preened as the others took off their flight packs.

"Man, that had to be one of the coolest experiences of my life!" Rumpus exclaimed.

"It was one of your grandfather's favorite things to do too." The lion turned around to the tree Agape sat in and pushed a large knot in the trunk. A secret door sprang open, revealing a closet full of supplies. "Your grandpa has several of these little hiding spots around the island. They come in handy to stash supplies—or hide in if you are in a jam." Rumpus noticed some tools hanging on the inside of the tree and a couple backpacks on the floor. "Throw your pack in there and start getting your cloak on," Leonidas instructed. "It's time to be really careful and cautious, kid. This port is a dangerous place, crawling with soldiers. Between them and the pirates, we have a lot to worry about."

Rumpus recalled now that he'd been told to come to this port by the walrus he had met at the

Resound Fields. "I can't believe I didn't remember this before, but this guy I met, Party Walrus, told me to come here when I first arrived."

The old lion stepped back in surprise. "Well, that changes things a little bit. Without question, THEY know you are here. That stupid walrus had to have called it in by now, or sent one of the messenger bees. He's not a bad dude—he used to be a sweet guy in his heart—but he was always angry and confused back in the day, which led to his breakdown. He did what THEY asked him to do, and he did it to survive, but his heart was always hurting deep down. THEY retired him only to keep him on as an informant and stationed him in that pond over by the Resound Fields. It had been years since anything happened around there. Party Walrus has a talent for getting people to reveal information, and then he passes it along." Leonidas scratched the mane below his chin. "I've partied with him here and there. I think the reason he cracked is that he craves doing the right thing, but just doesn't know how. Maybe the good guy will pop out one day, but for now we need to be careful. If he sent you here it was to help THEY, and he was hoping someone else would grab you for him."

Rumpus paused. "Don't you mean help them?"

Limerick Cove

"No, THEY," Leonidas explained. "The Tyrannical Helpers Eyeballing You. Everyone who works for the military is part of THEY."

The two of them cloaked up and told Agape to fly high and stay out of sight. As they ventured farther into the port, the population of creatures increased, with all sorts of merchants bringing the wildest things to sell and trade. A large bear walked next to them, carrying a wicker basket full of cupcakes with arms and legs. Leonidas noticed Rumpus looking at the basket and whispered, "When the cupcakes they release don't get consumed, they evolve arms and legs, along with sharper teeth. The arms and legs bring a whole different level of escape..." Leonidas shook his head. "Stay away from all of it, man. There is no breaking free if you go down that road."

They walked in silence; Rumpus noticed Agape here and there, flying high above as the streets became crowded. No one seemed to be paying attention to them at all. A wide gate provided entry to the port, and Rumpus noticed several creatures in uniforms. A couple had mean looking bees on leashes floating next to them; all were all playing cards on a large barrel.

"If you act like they are not there, Rumpus, then they will barely notice you either," Leonidas murmured.

"It's been so long since there has been any real action, the majority of the THEY soldiers don't even know what they do for a job. Most of them over-indulge on cupcake rations and were never that bright to begin with. That being said, we don't need to get too close. Stupid creatures tend to do irrational things." He put a paw on Rumpus's shoulder. "We are almost to the hut that sells the ink we are looking for."

The two travelers walked up to a long structure with a flip-up overhang. Leonidas placed his arm in front of Rumpus, signaling him to stand still farther away from the counter, while the lion continued forward to talk to the storekeeper. The store was crowded with all kinds of oddities and tools. Small creatures in cages and glass jars hung from the ceiling. Rumpus saw all kinds of strange tools, then noticed a plunger hanging up on the wall. Leonidas was chopping it up with the gruff storekeeper, so Rumpus focused in on the ink seller. The grumpy cephalopod stared at the rhino through his dirty glasses under fluffy, oversized

eyebrows. His translucent blue arms were changing colors toward redder tones, indicating his concern about a newcomer's face looking into his storefront.

"Why would you want that ink?" the storekeeper asked. "I would be happy to sell it to you, but that's an awfully expensive item that almost no one ever uses anymore." He gestured behind him with one of his octopus arms, catching a bottle with the suckers. "I could sell you this northern sand beetle ink, along with several other items, for the same price." He grinned at Rumpus. "What say you, my quiet friend? Do you not know how to speak?" One of the other eight arms pointed at the hooded rhino.

"He is a man of few words, but he knows what he wants," Leonidas cut in, putting his paws on the counter. "We are not here to buy a bunch of other things. All we would like is the ink, that bamboo pen, and no more sales pitches, if you don't mind."

"Ok, ok. Sorry. I was just trying to save you some money. I haven't sold that combo in years…" His eyes flashed to Rumpus suspiciously, as though he had just noticed the size of the large, cloaked

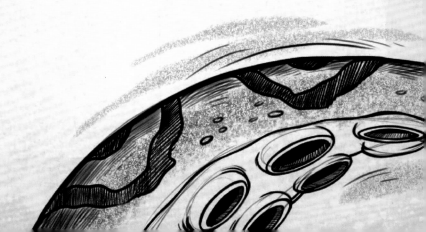

figure. "And this is all you need?" he hollered over to Rumpus.

Taking a step forward, Rumpus raised his arm and pointed at the plunger. As he did, his horn bumped the edge of the overhang and pulled back his cloak, revealing the tip of his snout. The storekeeper instantly noticed the horn and recalled who he'd sold the ink to last. One of his tentacles shook, handing the plunger labeled Two Ton over to Rumpus, while another handed the ink and pen to Leo. A third arm took the small sack of coins. They all moved in slow motion.

Leonidas noticed one of the octopus's eyes looking down to his side, where an old wanted poster of El Vaquero was pinned next to his register. Just as the lion realized the danger, a bell clanged in alarm, its rope pulled by one of the storekeeper's other tentacles. "Help! Help! It's El Vaquero!"

Leonidas grabbed his hood and pulled it off, yelling over to the shocked rhino. "Rumpus! It's time to get out of here. We need to run! Move! Move! Move!"

CHAPTER 15

PORT CROON AND THE BUFFOON PLATOON

Rumpus ran through the crowd like a bowling ball, knocking creatures down like pins. With a plunger in each hand hanging low, he wondered if he looked like one of those guys running with swords in an anime. Creatures were tossed through the air as Leo kept tucked down, running in the wake Rumpus left behind him.

Back at the merchant, a group of THEY guards arrived. The freaked-out octopus continued ringing the bell, shouting "El… El… El… El… El… El…"

A large, goofy-looking boar of a guard smacked him. "Get yourself together and stop ringing that damn bell," the guard screamed, spraying spit all over the shopkeeper's squishy face. "What is the problem?"

As the octopus finally said, "El Vaquero!" another guard yanked on his superior's arm, pointing in the direction of the large rhino and lion parting the crowd like a banana split. "Is that a rhino running through the crowd? There was a message from the general about a   rhino in the Resound Fields. That   must be him! After him!"

Rumors were known to spread around port like wildfire, and soon Rumpus and Leonidas had three soldiers chasing them—but others were descending on the market. Both soldiers and pirates joined in the chase. One group followed orders; the other group hoped to reap a reward, thinking that El Vaquero had returned to the island.

Leonidas yelled out to the charging rhino. "We're drawing a crowd!" But instead of offering a solution, the lion started laughing uncontrollably.

Rumpus wasn't amused by the laughter, but the more he thought about it, he kind of liked what was going on. Something about it all just felt right to him. He came sliding to a halt, causing Leo to slam into his back with a thud. "Where do we go, Leo?" he yelled at the lion unpeeling himself from his backside.

Before Leonidas had a chance to answer, a booming voice commanded them, "Just stop right where you are."

Rabbit soldiers and pirates and a large group of dumb onlookers—the type who gather to watch an accident and block traffic for everyone else—surrounded them on all sides.

"We order you to stop and come with us," shouted a lead guard. "Don't make us take you by force."

After his short rampage down the street, Rumpus felt big and not in the mood for orders. "And if we don't?" he replied.

The circle closed in on the rhino with two plungers and the lion with an angry bee eater sitting on his staff, all in an attack position. "Did the reward say 'dead or alive' on the poster?" called a bystander from the back as several of the pirates started to cackle.

The highest-ranking officer swung around with his clubs in hand. "If any of you lay a finger on them, you will answer to me." Turning back around, he pointed his baton at the duo.

Before he responded to Rumpus, another pirate voice interrupted from the back of the crowd. "Eat it, you saggy-butt, cupcake-eating landlubber! This be our catch of the day, as is the reward due to us."

Tension rose as some of the soldiers realized that if the pirates attacked, they'd have to face both criminals and a charging rhino. They shared nervous glances instead of watching the two causing the commotion.

The commander sensed the change and belted out an order. "Squad A, with me! You restrain the prisoners. The rest, clear out these dirty, salty dogs." He hollered behind into the crowd, "You lot clear out, or we will throw you in holding with no cupcakes!"

The crowd started to disperse when a bottle came crashing down on a soldier's helmets, sending the mob into a brawling frenzy. Rumpus and Leonidas dropped their defensive posture, staring at the scene unfolding around them when the commander—stepping on the torso of one of the pirates—caught sight of the pair looking for a way out. "Come here, you two!" he ordered.

Stepping in front of his older friend, the irritated rhino raised his plungers. "This one is mine, Leo." Rumpus rushed at the guard, fighting plunger to baton. The large rabbit swung for Rumpus's head, causing the rhino to bend backward as it swished by his face. While he wasn't looking, the commander's left hand stabbed the other baton onto his stomach, sending him down onto one knee. The two stared at each other for a moment in the chaos, and Rumpus adjusted his grip on the plungers while the rabbit in front of him smirked. Just as the commander started to charge him, Rumpus pushed up off his one knee, preparing for the worst. Suddenly, Leo stepped in the way, jamming the end of his staff into the rabbit's gut, lifting him up in the air, and flipping him up and over his back. "Rumpus, we need a path out of this ring of fire. Can you do that?"

Rumpus glanced at the rabbit flying over him before looking back at the crowd. Now a pirate was coming straight at him. Rumpus was ready to charge—and charge he did. Launching forward, he swung a plunger like a backhand. The rubber end connected with the pirate's jaw and sent him flying. At the same time, Rumpus stuffed his right plunger into the face of another soldier, suctioning his jaw and throwing him to the ground. He pushed forward and heard Leonidas behind him yelling, "That's it! You got this!" Rumpus dropped his shoulder, crashing into the brawl surrounding him.

From a bird's view high above, it looked like this: all the soldiers and pirates flew back like someone throwing cards in the air. Rumpus swung his plungers and Leo swung his staff, throwing brawlers out of the crowd, while Agape pecked on the heads of fighters who stayed standing. The rampaging rhino broke through the dusty doughnut cloud of swinging arms and legs with Leo close behind him. The two started to get away from the battle when some of the brawlers noticed their reward was escaping.

"Hey! Hey! They're getting away!"

Soldiers biting arms and legs and pirates with fingers in noses slowed to stop. The group looked in the direction of the trail of dust.

"They're getting away!" screamed the commander.

The brawlers stopped fighting and started pushing each other out of the way to race after the fugitives.

Something had snapped in Rumpus. He felt like he was in his element more than he had ever felt back in Kansas City. Even though he was extremely worried about his current situation, an intense connection to his grandfather improved his courage. A big grin came over his face as a couple rabbits charged toward them from the outside of town. A horde of soldiers and pirates chased after them.

Close behind Rumpus was a gleeful lion remembering his times with El Vaquero. Above, Agape glided back and forth. The group was coming up on the last row of shops and carts before the edge of the woods, and Rumpus's only plan was to get into the trees and hide. It was too bad the tree they'd thrown the gliders in wasn't big enough to hide them, and Rumpus wasn't sure if they could get there and get the packs on quickly enough. He could hear some of the brood behind tripping and grasping at his lion partner. He decided it was time to stop running, so he slid in the dirty cobblestoned street. His shoulders connected with the two soldiers ahead, sending them flying over the shops and the beginning of the tree line behind them. Spinning around, Rumpus caught Leo in his arms, and the crowd of pursuers came to a screeching halt with the pirate in the front circling his arms as if he could stop the world from crashing down.

The group stumbled over each other like a wave or rockslide. "I got a way to get us out of here, Rumpus!" yelled out the lion. Agape flew down, landing on Rumpus's shoulder, and they once again squared off against their foes in a staring contest. Leo whispered, "It's going to take a minute, but when I blow this whistle, Sunny will find us and help out." The old lion reached into his mane, where he grasped a small, hidden whistle hanging around his neck on a leather string. The mob closed in as Leonidas put the whistle to his lips and pushed out a blow. Rumpus didn't hear anything, but to the mob around him, it sounded like a dozen high pitched train whistles. They all grabbed their ears, many dropping to their knees or onto their backs. "It's now or never, Rumpus!" Leonidas yelled back at him. "I need you to clear a way again so we can meet up with Sunny." Rumpus, a little confused by the fact that he didn't hear anything, stepped forward, plunging a soldier's face on his right and a pirate's face on his left. He yanked down, throwing both of them to the ground. Then he continued forward, swinging his plungers and clearing a path while picking up momentum.

The creatures of the port continued to watch from the sidelines and from windows as alarm bells rang all around them, but Rumpus noticed some of the inhabitants cheering him on. Soldiers and pirates climbed over each other, some finding their feet to chase Rumpus again. Agape zigzagged above through the crowd. Rumpus followed her back to the port's edge where the ships docked. Occasionally Rumpus would stop and turn around to fight some of their pursuers, then continue to run, catching up to Leonidas. He heard someone cheer, "Vaquero!" and others yelling, "Get him!" He realized that being the guys slamming into carts and climbing up on top of businesses probably wasn't the best way to make friends.

He could see ships now, and a loud screech above him drew his attention up. It was Sunny! "Get to the docks, and we'll get you out of here!" the griffin called.

Emboldened with the idea that he was going to really get out of this place, Rumpus picked up speed and caught up to Leo. As they ran, Rumpus handed Leonidas the two plungers and scooped the lion up onto his back. The old sage started laughing. "Just like old times!" he said with glee.

Rumpus followed Agape to the docks, where he could see Sunny flying in circles. They were almost there, but the mob was just steps behind them, with Leo bopping the closest on their heads with a plunger to slow them down a bit. "When you get to the dock, Rumpus, you need to run to the end and jump," Leo coached. "Sunny will take care of the rest. You can do this!"

They made it to the beginning of the dock and the horde just ahead of the pirates and soldiers grasping for Leonidas as he rode on the rhino's back. Pirates jumped off their ships and ran down the dock, adding to chase.

Leonidas used one of the plungers to gesture to a large cage made of twisted sticks full of fully grown, mean, and evolved cupcakes. "Grab the cage as you run by, Rumpus, and break it!"

Rumpus nodded and reached out with his right hand, snagging the cage. A wild cupcake instantly bit his hand, causing him to jerk the side of the little

prison so hard that it broke apart. About fifty rabid, sweet treats swarmed onto the dock. The cupcakes rushed into the mob, adding a chaotic mess of biting to the confused brawl. Rumpus didn't even bother to look back, instead running toward his griffin friend. They made it to the end of the dock, and he pulled Leonidas off his back and tossed him up toward Sunny. The lion landed on the griffin's back as he flew by.

"I'll get you on my next pass!" Sunny called.

Rumpus turned his attention back to the sugar-infused ball of violence just in time to see the smash of a flying land speeder plow through the

THE WORST...

crowd, sending frosting, pirates, and soldiers in every direction. It swung to the side, and a vicious looking rabbit with a curly mustache lunged off the cycle toward Rumpus, batons in each hand. Two more soldiers in red uniforms on their own mini-cycles quickly unmounted and got into a defensive position.

General Von Hareliar had arrived!

Rumpus locked eyes with the general for a moment before the angry rabbit barreled down on him. The slow-motion silence of the run was broken by Leo yelling, "Jump Rumpus, JUMP!!"

Rumpus didn't even think. He trusted his new friends, so he turned around and leapt off the high dock, arms stretched out toward the horizon line over the water.

He couldn't even see where Sunny was. Below him, translucent teal water shone out to the horizon. Suddenly, two large talons grabbed his wrists, and he was swinging up as they climbed. His vision went from the water to nothing but clouds. A thrown baton spun by him as they turned back toward land. The general was standing on the dock, jumping up and down and screaming. They swooped over him, and Leonidas sang out a greeting. "Good morning, General. It's been a while, haha!"

Sunny climbed back up, and Rumpus could faintly hear the general. "I'll have you soon, just like the last rhino that didn't know his place!"

Rumpus looked back in anger. What did that mean? Like the last rhino? The four of them flew over the port shops, where the inhabitants below looked up in awe. Sunny started to swing Rumpus back and forth until he swung him so hard that he did a backflip and landed on Sunny's back. Rumpus gripped for dear life, and his lion friend sitting in front of him laughed.

"Put these plungers in that backpack, son. We're heading back to the fields to regroup and find you a place to lay low. There's no hiding the fact that you are here now."

Rumpus nodded and started to put his plungers away. At the edge of the port, just before they hit the tree line, he saw Party Walrus looking up at them, his mouth slack jawed. All Rumpus could do as they passed by was point at the walrus. He knew if he'd gone the way the walrus had told him to, he would probably be captured. As the port faded behind them, he finally sighed in relief. Sunny then followed the river along the base of the mountains toward the place that had started it all for Rumpus.

CHAPTER 16

DJ, CAN I MAKE A REQUEST?

Hours later, the exhausted griffin flew over the pond where Rumpus had originally met Party Walrus, making their way to the center of the Resound Fields where Sheol had dropped the rhino off. The group landed, and the two adventurers dismounted. Leonidas stretched as Agape found a small branch sticking out of the ground and used it to clean his feathers.

"Well, that was just plain crazy," said the old lion as he sat down cross-legged.

"Something tells me you knew full well there was a big chance that was how it was all going to go down," Sunny scolded, sitting down in the circle. "Why did you guys go to Port Croon?"

Leonidas closed his eyes and tilted his face back to soak up the sun. "You may think I knew what was going to happen, and maybe I did, but it was Rumpus who wanted to get some of the ink and the same pen his grandfather used. You know the rules, Sunny…we don't stop what is supposed to happen."

Rumpus felt frustrated—or maybe he was just exhausted by it all. "You could have at least warned me, you cooky old lion."

"Where's that faith that caused you to jump off that dock without even looking?" Leonidas asked. "It may have been a little scary, but you seemed to be in your element, my friend. Personally, I think you found yourself today, and it was worth it to take the risk." The old lion shrugged. "I believe we would have been fine no matter what."

Rumpus pulled off his backpack and slid out the field guide with his new ink and pen. Without even looking or opening his eyes, the Leonidas spoke again. "The back of the pen is where the ink goes in. The top of the bottle comes off, exposing a thin spout that fits in there perfectly. Fill the pen up and draw in that book for a minute while we rest. You earned it. Maybe we can see if you can bring drawings to life too."

The tired rhino felt a little bit of pressure. What if it didn't work for him? What if all of that had been a waste of time, and he was nothing like his grandfather? Leo was right though. Where was that faith now? So Rumpus filled the pen and opened the field guide to the next open page. He stared at the page for a minute, then looked around at the rest of his team. They were all basking in the sun, enjoying the sound of the sweet breeze flowing through the buffalo grass.

This time Sunny broke the silence. "I love this place, even though music hasn't been heard here in years. It seems to still have some of the leftover peace from those concerts years ago, before they were outlawed and the record players were smashed. This place used to be the center of our life."

"Sounds nice," Rumpus told the majestic griffin. "Some of my good friends back home are DJs. In KC, they would transport people away from their troubles too."

"Sounds familiar, doesn't it, Sunny?" asked Leonidas. The old lion kept his face tilted to the suns. "So, what do you think you are going to draw first?" he asked Rumpus.

The rhino looked down at the blank page and paused. "I have an idea, but it might be a little ambitious."

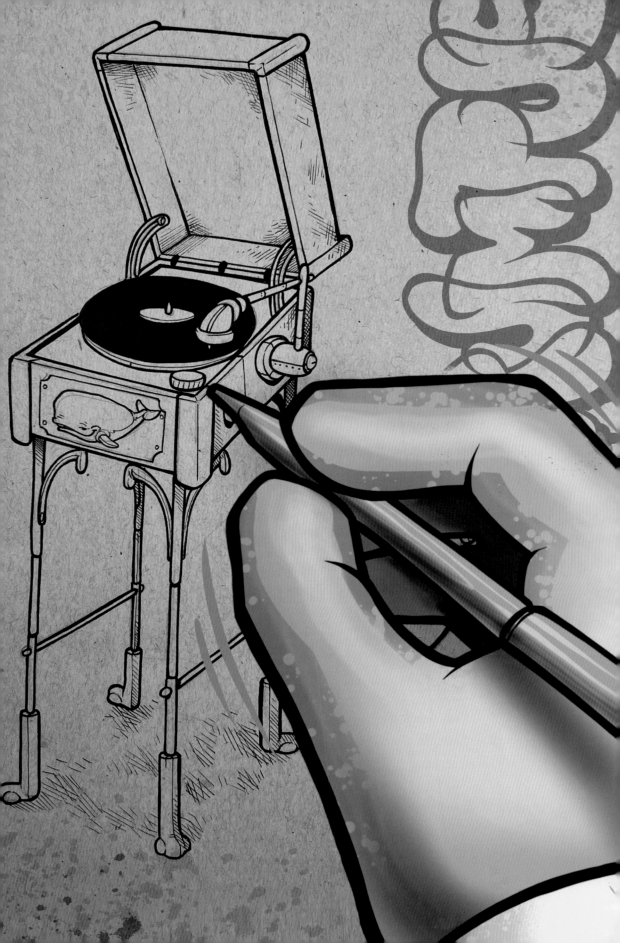

Sunny stood up and walked over, leaning on Rumpus's shoulder. Her hot breath smelled like pancakes with whipped cream, and with a gentle nudge, she spoke. "Don't put so much pressure on yourself to perform. Just like any drawing you may have ever done in the past, do something that inspires you, and make it from the heart. If drawing it into existence doesn't work out today, then it is what it is. The most important thing is that you enjoy what you are doing." Sunny moved off to the side and lay down in the grass. "Take your time, Rumpus. We're just going to hang out for a bit and wait for one of our friends. He'll take us in for the night."

Rumpus started sketching while the rest of the gang napped. He thought about his adventures so far. He thought about what he had witnessed that the residents of the island had been dealing with, and he thought about General Von Hareliar and his last words—getting him like the last rhino. His scribbles got more intense, and toward the end of his sketch, he started to smile. He was excited to show his new friends what he'd drawn, and when he was finished, he capped the pen with a POP! Rumpus blew on the page to make the ink dry faster.

The pop of the pen woke the crew up, and Leonidas leaned over to see what Rumpus had drawn. "Well, look at that," the lion mused. "That's amazing, Rumpus. It's different from what we have seen before, but there is no getting confused about what that is."

Sunny wandered over and peered into the book. "Oh my, I love it. What a great idea."

As they talked about the newly imagined drawing of a turntable, another voice spoke up in front of them. "Man, what we could do with that in these fields."

Rumpus looked up to see the creature he'd first met after getting spat out by Sheol, now standing in front of them. "I wonder what would happen if you tried to give that sketch a grab with your fingers and see if you could pull it out?"

Everyone agreed and urged Rumpus to give it a try. Agape nudged his shoulders, encouraging him.

"Wait, wait, wait... I don't even know what to do!"

"It's nothing to stress out over, Rumpus," Leonidas comforted. "You put a lot of thought into that being your first drawing in the field guide. Just concentrate, show some of that faith you have, and give it a shot. If now isn't the time, you have friends around you that are not worried about it. That may have been your grandpa's thing, and everyone is different." The lion grinned. "This should always be fun, Rumpus."

Rumpus looked down at the page and took a deep breath, filling his chest and exhaling really slowly. He placed his fingers on each side of the sketch. He wasn't even sure if he was doing it right, but it didn't hurt to try this way. Closing his eyes, Rumpus pictured the turntable being used—and how much it would upset the general and his army. This idea really made him smile. It made sense that his grandpa had worked at being a thorn in their side. He wanted to do the same.

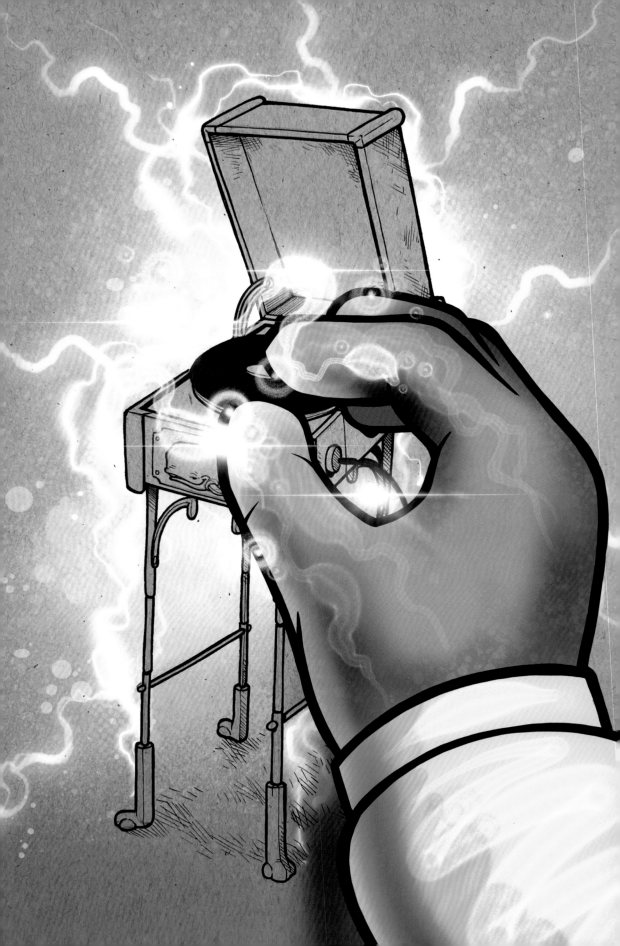

His fingers began to tingle, and light started to radiate around the edges of the drawing.

"Well, would you look at that," said the old lion. Rumpus opened his eyes to see that the sketch was peeling off the page. He gripped it tightly and, with eyes wide open, pulled the rest until his other arm reached under the turntable and scooped it out. The team cheered and patted him on the back while a tear rolled down his cheek. At that moment he felt a real connection with his grandfather, and he was blown away.

He turned around to the creature, his first encounter on the island, and said, "I think this needs to go to you. It's time to bring some music back to the fields. It sounds like it is something I really need to see and hear." As he started to hand over the turntable, he realized something. "By the way, I don't even think I ever got your real name."

The creature was grinning from ear to ear and looked back up to Rumpus, eyes watering. "My name is Harmonium. I can't tell you how happy and honored I am that you did this for the fields. It's been so many years."

Harmonium turned his attention to the turntable in his hand. Rumpus had drawn something similar to what his friends used, but also added things from his own imagination.

Rumpus spoke up. "If it works the way I imagined it, you need to start by holding out your arms and pressing the button over on the left side."

Smiling happily, Harmonium followed the instructions and pushed the button. A set of steampunk-looking legs sprang out from the sides, holding it up like a small table, and two cables popped out of the front and plugged themselves into the ground. The DJ was so excited. A small hum vibrated around them, as if all the grass had turned into millions of miniature speakers. Harmonium lifted the turntable arm and gently placed the needle on the record Rumpus had also drawn in the sketch. The snaps and crackle of the open air on the record popped all around them in surround sound. Then a gentle bass line faded in, followed by a guitar over a chill hop beat. Sound waves moved in a circular motion, swaying the tall buffalo grass around them. Rumpus dropped to his knees. He was overwhelmed by the saturation of the colors getting even richer, along with the most incredible sense of peace he had ever felt. All of

them stood in awe. The birds stopped singing, and animals and creatures of the fields stood, trying to figure out what was happening. Some of them had never heard music before.

The song came to a close, and the arm automatically returned to a resting position. The group looked at each other, acknowledging the moment. Rumpus spoke up first. "If that is what the fields used to be like…then I get it now."

Harmonium looked back at Rumpus, then turned his eyes back to the record. His large hands gently caressed the sides, moving it back and forth. Some creatures were now close to them, wondering if there was going to be another song. Bees flew above the grass, keeping an eye on them.

"We have some guests," sighed Sunny, "and it won't be long before some of those bees get word back to one of the outposts that we are here." She flapped her wings in concern. "I suggest we figure out where we are going soon."

Rumpus looked around and saw that they had guests hoping for more. "Back home it can be a little annoying to make a request of a DJ, but is it possible that I could make a request?"

The humbled DJ wasted no time in answering, "Anything for you, brother!"

The rhino closed his sketchbook and started putting it back into his bag. "Could you play that song one more time before we leave? I think there are some here that could really use it right now."

Without hesitation, Harmonium grabbed the record player arm and set it on the record again, singing "Myyyy pleaaasurrre!"

The song started to play, and Rumpus looked out over the fields at some of the creatures. He scanned the landscape, panning to the right when a large mass caught his attention in his peripheral vision. It was Sheol, floating over the tall grass fields with his eyes closed in bliss. The fields glowed even brighter than before.

Something was different this time the song played. It wasn't as foreign, and the creatures in the area closed their eyes in peace. The electricity traveled through the earth, sending both visual signals to the cameras and audio to the speakers in the different towns across the island. It transmitted everywhere there was an ear to hear—which included the general's.

General Von Hareliar was still in the town of Port Croon, waiting on information from his spies and looking over the destruction, when the music came through a speaker high up on a pole. The inhabitants around him fixed on nearly forgotten sounds not heard in years. Just as the general started screaming to his two guards to fetch his hover cycle, he noticed Party Walrus staring at the speaker too. "You!" he barked, pointing his baton at Walrusamus. But the walrus didn't hear him at all.

Just then a bee flew up and started chattering the news to the general that Rumpus was in the Resound Fields, with both a turntable and Sheol the whale. General Von Hareliar forgot about the walrus and mounted his hover cycle. "The boss is going to crush me if I don't get this squashed right away," he muttered. "Guards, follow me to the fields!"

The trio rushed off on their long journey back to Resound Fields.

In the middle of the island, the song came to an end, and Agape chased off the last couple of bees spying on them.

"It's time to go, guys," said Leonidas. "There is no way this went unnoticed, and it won't be happening again if we get caught today."

Harmonium pushed the button on the left side again, and this time the turntable closed up into a backpack he was able to throw onto his back. Looking over to Rumpus, he asked, "Do you want to go home? With Sheol here, we might be able to ask him."

Rumpus looked back over to the whale and thought about it for a moment. He wondered if it was his last chance. He also wondered if his grandpa was somewhere on the island, or, if he was gone, who might have gotten to him.

What was Rumpus going to go back to? A job he hated and that strange dream he lived in? He made his decision.

"I'm going to stay, if that is OK with you guys," Rumpus announced, "but I could use your help."

He waved to Sheol, who knew the answer. In a blip, the whale sucked into himself, leaving nothing but his mouth floating and his lips puckered into a kissing puss. With a loud smack, that disappeared too.

Sunny flew up into the air. "Until the next time, guys! With the way you get into trouble, I expect that I will be seeing you soon, haha!" The griffin climbed into the clouds until he vanished.

Harmonium looked at Leonidas, Rumpus, and Agape. "Come with me, guys. I got a killer ramen spot and a place to sleep tonight. Let's hit the road before THEY show up!"

Off the adventurers went down the road, talking happily about all the adventures they knew they were headed for.

THE END
(for now)

In the following
pages is a variety of
artwork and extras that
were created along
the way. Enjoy!

Alisa Ross - @40threads

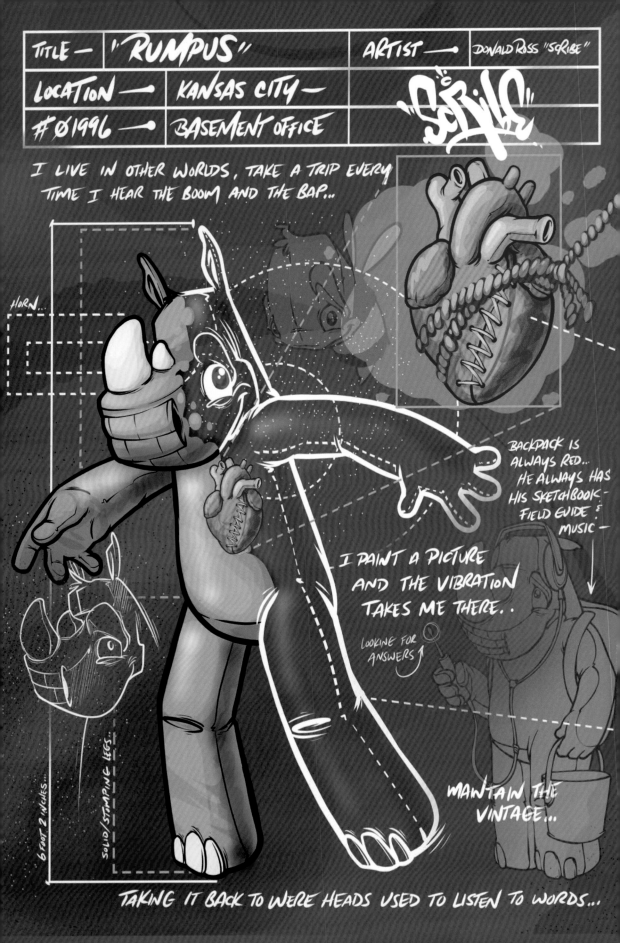

EMIT - @emit_df x scribe

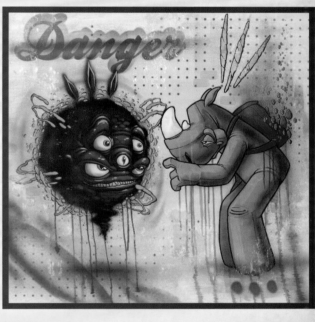

Photo by Philip Koenig

scribe x EMIT - @emit_df

Alisa Ross - @40threads

scribe x EMIT - @emi_df

Samuel -Produced by Okedoki - @okedoki_studio

Emit x Sub x Tuke x Scribe - @emit_df - @tonycuranaj - @tukeone - @scribeswalk

scribe x QUISP - @gearatt

Produced by UVD Toys
@uvdtoys

Alisa Ross @40threads

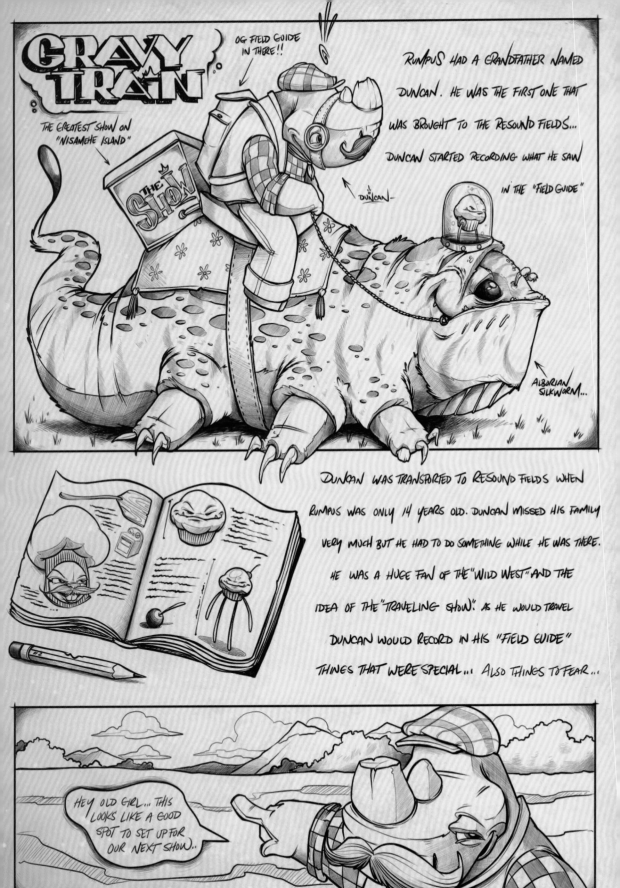

DUNCAN WOULD CAREFULLY PICK OUT A SPECIAL SPOT FOR HIS SHOW. IN HIS BOX HE KEPT 42 POSSIBLE SHOWS...

YOU SEE... DUNCAN HAD OBSERVED ALMOST EVERY PART OF NISAMEHE ISLAND AND HE WOULD SKETCH THE SPECIAL THINGS HE SAW IN THE DIFFERENT REGIONS. ONE DAY HE CRUMPLED UP A SKETCH, THREW IT ON THE GROUND NEXT TO HIM AND WHEN IT HIT THE DIRT... IT TURNED INTO A SMALL BEAN.

THAT'S JUST CRAZY...

THE

THAT BEAN ROLLED INTO A PUDDLE AND **POOF!**... IT TURNED INTO A LIVE VERSION OF HIS SKETCH! WAS IT BECAUSE HIS PENCIL WAS MADE FROM THE GIVERS TREE? WHO KNOWS? TODAY DUNCAN IS ADDING WATER TO HIS FAVORITE SKETCH... SKETCH #22

TINY BIT OF WATER

22

SKETCH #22 WAS A TRIO
ACTUALLY CALLED CATCH22!
JKR7Ø
TRYSTYL
&
ICY ROC
&

JKR7Ø WOULD GATHER SOUNDS
FROM THE AREA FOR LOOPS —
TRYSTYL WOULD MIX , FLIP,
AND MASTER THE SOUNDS
ACROSS THE FIELDS ....
AND ICY ROC WOULD
MASSAGE THE SOUNDS INTO A COOL
BREEZE COOLING OFF THE FIELDS —

JKR7Ø

"TRYSTYL"...

ICY ROC...

THE TRIO WOULD LET THIER RYTHUMS DANCE ACROSS THE FIELDS AND EVERY ANIMAL IN THE RESOUND FIELDS WOULD END UP SITTING IN THE COOL BREEZE. THEY WOULD BECOME REFRESHED, IMMERSED IN A "LOVE" THAT WAS IMPOSSIBLE TO PUT INTO WORDS. AFTER HOURS OF RESOUNDING FREEDOM DUNCAN WOULD PULL OUT HIS SKETCHBOOK...

AS HE WOULD SKETCH THE GROUP, BOTH THE MUSIC AND TRIO WOULD FADE BACK INTO THE PAGES. DUNCAN WOULD PACK UP... AND HEAD TO HIS NEXT SHOW.